COLLEGE BOYS

COLLEGE BOYS

GAY EROTIC STORIES

EDITED BY
SHANE ALLISON

Cleis Press Inc., 2246 Sixth St., Berkeley, California 94710.

Printed in the United States.
Cover design: Scott Idleman
Cover photograph: Ryan McVay/Getty Images
Text design: Frank Wiedemann
Cleis logo art: Juana Alicia
ISBN-13: 978-1-573-44399-9

"Glory Hole Surprise" © 2009 by Shane Allison first appeared in *Mandate*. "My Seven-Inch Toy" © 2009 by Donald Ammer first appeared in *Mandate*. "Dorm" © 2009 by Tom Cardamone first appeared online in Clean Sheets. "College Dive Bar, 1:00 A.M." by Natty Soltesz first appeared in *Freshmen* © 2009. "Confessions of a College Sex Slave" © 2009 by Aaron Travis first appeared in *Manscape*. "Frat-napped" © 2009 by Logan Zachary first appeared in *Taken by Force* edited by Christopher Pierce.

Contents

INTRODUCTION
BIG MEN
ON CAMPUS

The best thing about living in a college town is the smoking-hot college boys that descend upon it every semester. Some return to continue their studies while cruising for the next lay, while the fresh meat touch, feel and suck their way around their new world of higher education. I think of fraternity houses filled to the brim with boys. I refuse to believe that there isn't *something* going on in secret behind those bedroom doors. It's been nine years since my own exit from university. I admit that I've secretly lusted after more than a few of my professors, thinking of their lips pressed against my own, among other things. I picture Clark as I write this, the adorable football jock who sat in front of me in Modern Poetry, whose dirty blond spiked hair I wanted to feel on my bare chest, or Ryan, the bookish brunet whose kisses I wanted to taste, as well as a whole plethora of boys who teased with their lithe, sweaty brawn and million-dollar smiles.

What is it about college guys that set our loins so feverishly on fire?

In this volume I have gathered some of the best writers of erotica to share their stories of hot college high jinks. Aaron Travis kicks it off in "Confessions of a College Sex Slave," with an eager-to-please bottom boy antagonist who lusts after his sexy, demanding roommate.

The tables are turned when a professor is schooled on the ins and outs of autofellatio by a student most willing to teach in Rob Rosen's "Self-Taught." Neil Plakcy heats up the pages with his tale of a twinkish crew member on a rowing team who fawns over another in "Coxed." A frat boy wannabe gets in over his head in Logan Zachary's "Frat-napped." If you're as avid a fan of the collegiate kind as I am, you're going to love the stories woven by these salacious, raunchy bards of gay erotica, so sit or lie back and enjoy. I know I did.

Shane Allison

CONFESSIONS OF A COLLEGE SEX SLAVE

Aaron Travis

I want to tell you about the master/slave relationship I had with my college roommate for two years.

Doug and I started rooming together off-campus during my sophomore year. Doug was a junior. This was at an East Coast Ivy League college. We had grown up in the same city, gone to the same high school and known each other as acquaintances for years. I had always admired Doug and I guess I had something of a crush on him from a distance. He was very competitive and athletic, very bright and popular. He was one of the best-looking guys I've ever known, tall and muscular with wavy brown hair and a superb natural physique. He also had the biggest cock I've ever sucked.

We ended up sharing an apartment with separate bedrooms out of mutual convenience, not friendship. Like I said, we were really just acquaintances. Friends who knew we were both looking for a roommate matched us up.

I was pretty intimidated about living with him. Doug was

way out of my league in every way. Whenever we were alone together I'd get nervous and act stupid. I knew he had me pegged as a real weenie, and he didn't hide it. He snubbed me in lots of little ways, never inviting me along when he'd go out drinking with friends, never making any real effort to put me at ease.

Meanwhile I just kept getting more and more of a crush on him, fueled by the torture of seeing him practically naked around the apartment every day. He liked to relax wearing just a pair of tight nylon gym shorts. I could see he had a big cock. He also had the kind of perfect body you see in underwear ads—broad chest and shoulders, narrow hips, a washboard stomach. At night when he'd go out I'd lie in bed, thinking about him and masturbating.

The first time we did anything was one night when he came in pretty drunk after a date with his then-girlfriend, Dee. Dee was something of a bitch—even Doug said so. The only reason he dated her was because she looked like a fashion model and came from a rich family. Doug was always very conscious of his own high social standing, and it was important that he be seen with the "right kind" of woman.

But Dee absolutely would not put out. Apparently she wouldn't even give him a hand-job. That night he came in tight and horny. I remember he was wearing a jacket and a tie he'd loosened around his collar. I'd been up late, reading in the living room. He sat by me on the sofa, flipped on the TV, drank a beer and made small talk. He'd never done anything even that sociable with me before. I was flattered, flustered, and very horny for him. I guess he could tell. After a while, completely out of the blue, he said: "Tom's been telling all the guys that you suck cock. Is that right?"

Tom was another mutual acquaintance. How he could have known that I had dropped in at the tearooms on campus a few times beginning that semester, I don't know; maybe Doug just made it up to flush me out. I don't remember answering, but the next thing I knew Doug had his pants unzipped and was holding his cock straight up in his fist, hard as a rock.

I was absolutely blown away. It was the most beautiful thing I'd ever seen, like a true work of art. Not every cock is attractive, even big ones. But Doug's cock was the most beautiful piece of meat I've ever seen, before or since. It was easily eight inches long and thick as a baseball bat, with a smooth, polished crown. By the glow of the TV set it had a marblelike shine, very sleek and smooth.

I leaned over and started sucking it. Pretty soon I was on my knees between his legs, feasting on his cock in a kind of ecstasy. He leaned back on the sofa and let me suck to my heart's content. He came twice in my mouth, without me pulling off and without his cock getting soft.

Afterward, he said something about "good job" and went into his bedroom and closed the door.

After that, nothing really changed between us except the sex. Doug stayed just as distant as before, and there was no indication that he liked me any better than he ever had. But he was quite willing to let me suck his cock when it pleased him. We fell into a regular schedule, mainly around his dates with Dee. I guess it was less frustrating if he was already satisfied when he went out with her, because he would always have me suck him off right before he'd pick her up. Then when he'd come in later he'd have me suck him off again. The second time was usually better, for me at least, because he'd be a little tight, and he'd let loose more, getting into it and really throwing a good, hard fuck into my face. I think maybe he'd feel a little hostile about Dee not letting him get into her pants, and take it out on me. By degrees he got rougher and rougher. I never complained, and I'm sure he could tell that I liked it. He'd intentionally make me gag, pull out his cock and slap me with it, sometimes call me names like cocksucker and bitch.

I was usually naked when I sucked him off. I could see it coming, and I'd arrange to be wearing just my robe or underwear when we'd start, and then slip them off. He'd be fully dressed before going out on a date, and I liked sucking his big cock through the fly of his dress slacks, with him standing over me in a jacket and tie while I groveled naked on the floor between his legs. When he'd come in later he'd usually strip down some, though he usually left at least his undershirt on. There was something that really excited me about being naked and subservient while he stayed dressed or casually stripped-down and fed me his cock.

If it sounds like I didn't have much of a social life of my own, that was the case. I became more and more obsessed with Doug, and as long as he was willing to let me suck his big cock on a regular basis I had no real desire to go out looking for anything else. I never resented staying in and waiting up for him on weekend nights, knowing that he would be in later to give me what I was craving. Between Doug and a heavy academic load, I was completely busy and completely satisfied.

This situation went on all through the fall term. Things didn't really change until after Christmas break. Holidays can always be depressing, and they're especially confusing when you're in college and find yourself back in a home situation away from your normal routine. I guess I was even more obsessed with Doug than I'd realized, and got very nervous and upset after not seeing him for almost a month. He'd made big plans for the holidays, going skiing with his family, and taking Dee along, while I spent a miserable time with my mother and father, bored and frustrated. (It occurs to me that Doug may have gotten horny and frustrated over the holidays, too, which would explain why things were so volatile on both sides when we returned to school after break.)

I was dying to suck Doug off from the minute he walked into the apartment. I didn't have the confidence to make the first move, and instead acted sullen and hurt. He ignored me, until that weekend when he had a date with Dee. Then he expected me to get down on my knees on cue. Instead, something clicked inside me and I started threatening him, saying I was going to tell Dee and all his other friends about us.

Doug got very cold. He claimed that he'd already told them, including Dee, that he suspected I was some kind of faggot, that I was a little unhinged and probably had a crush on him and the only reason he stayed with me was because he felt sorry for me. In other words, I could go ahead and tell them anything and I'd just be making a fool of myself. He also made it very clear that he didn't give a damn about me and just considered me a convenient hole to unload in, and since I was pulling such a stunt I could forget about giving him blow jobs from then on.

He left for his date with Dee. I was miserable all night. When he came in I was waiting on the sofa, wearing my underwear. He went straight into his room and shut the door.

This went on for about a month. I was a wreck. Doug showed absolutely no signs of strain. I started believing that I meant nothing to him, or next to nothing, and he could take me or leave me. I think now that he was just manipulating me into doing what he wanted.

One night when he came in late I was in such a state that I started pleading with him, really letting it out, telling him I was in love with him. He became very surly and abusive, shoving me around (physically he was a lot stronger and heavier than me), calling me names. It was an ugly, humiliating situation. It was also charged with sex. It ended with him pushing me down on the floor and telling me to take off my underwear. He sat in a chair across the room and told me to crawl across the carpet on my hands and knees. When I got there he made me kiss his shoes. He pulled off his belt and started slapping it against my ass. I was amazed at how much it hurt and more amazed at how much it turned me on. I remember burying my face in his crotch, only to have him pull my hair and slap my face away, telling me to beg for it. That was the first time (but far from the last) that I begged out loud to suck Doug's cock.

He was much rougher with me that night than he'd ever been before. From then on the sex stayed just as rough. He got a kick out of making me beg. He especially seemed to like slapping me with his cock and using his belt on me.

After that night we pretty much had sex whenever he wanted it. We still did it on the nights he'd go out, but he'd also make me suck him off on a whim, when he was stepping out of the shower or just getting in from classes. Whenever Doug wanted his big, beautiful cock serviced, all he had to do was snap his fingers and I'd come crawling on my hands and knees.

We never actually slept together in the same bed. His bedroom was off-limits. Our sex was always in the living room, and afterward I'd end up alone in my own bed for the night.

When he'd have friends over it was the same as always, with me hovering uninvited in the background—just a roommate, not a friend. I began to have a recurrent fantasy, part dread and part wishfulness, that he would make me suck him off in front of his buddies.

At the end of the semester we both signed a rental agreement to share the apartment again the next fall. The afternoon he was supposed to leave for home I made special plans to be there, and I had fantasies about giving him a farewell blow job for the summer. But when I got in from my last final exam, he'd already packed and left early. He didn't even leave me a note.

I spent a long, hot summer with my parents, working part-time. The only thing that made it bearable was knowing I'd be seeing Doug again in the fall. I managed to have some sex by hanging out at a seedy porn peep show and at some local gay bars, but nothing came along that was even remotely interesting enough to distract me from my obsession with Doug. I had his parents' address and wrote him a couple of letters, not saying much for fear that someone else might read them. Even so, I agonized over every word, trying to let him know how much I missed him without sounding too servile. I even called a couple of times, but hung up before anyone could answer.

Doug spent the summer traveling, with one long trip to Europe with his older brother and another trip camping with his family in Utah and Arizona. The rest of the time he spent swimming and pumping weights in the gym at his folks' country club. He never even sent me a postcard.

But urges must have been building up inside him all summer, because the day we both got back to the apartment for fall semester, something exploded. My parents dropped me off and helped carry in luggage while Doug sat leafing through a magazine on the sofa. As soon as they left, he got up, walked over and slapped me hard across the face. He told me to get out of my clothes and get on the floor where I belonged.

I remember I went hard as a rock the instant he slapped me. After that I did everything he told me to. For the first time he started working over my nipples, being extremely rough with them. I'd never had my tits played with before, and the pain was almost more than I could take. He used his belt on me, making me bend over and grab my ankles. He'd grab a fistful of my hair and pull me upright and punch me in the belly, then make me bend over while he whipped my ass some more.

That was the first time he ever fucked me. He was all ready

for it, with a jar of lubricant and some rubbers. Before he did it he put some clothespins on my nipples and a black dog collar around my neck. I was excited out of my mind. He did it first with me bent over the sofa. I'd only been fucked a couple of times before and didn't really know how to relax, and Doug had a very big cock. It hurt like hell. Afterward he made me suck him off some more and fucked me again, using the belt on me while he did it. We had sex off and on all through the afternoon and evening. I was completely exhausted and slept until after two the next day.

Obviously, Doug had learned a few things over the summer. He eventually told me he had had an ongoing affair with a bartender at his parents' country club, an older guy in his late twenties who had more or less become Doug's sex slave for the summer. I remember feeling jealous and hurt about his having had something that serious with another guy, but at the same time I was on fire with excitement at the new things that Doug was doing to me.

That semester I was absolutely Doug's slave. The sex was relentless. It was also very rough, bordering sometimes on brutal. The meaner he got, the more submissive I became. The more servile I behaved, the more encouraged he was to keep pushing me. The humiliation was not just physical. He would say embarrassing things about me to his friends while I was in the room. He treated me like his personal servant around the apartment. He never showed the least sign of weakness or vulnerability with me. He was always very cold and very demanding.

His demands became more extreme and bizarre. Unless he was expecting company, around the apartment I was allowed to wear nothing but a dog collar. Some days he would make me put a plug up my ass before I left for classes. He began to keep me in bondage at night, not only to have sex but simply for his amusement. I remember him relaxing and watching TV or talking on the phone while I stood nude in the corner, with my hands cuffed behind me and my ankles strapped together. Occasionally he would get up for something and punch me in the belly as he walked by, or slap me across the face, or push me down and yell at me to get back up again. I lived for the nights he would fuck me or let me suck his big cock. Sometimes I would suck it for hours while he sprawled on the sofa watching bisex porn DVDs on his new flat-screen TV and I squatted on my knees between his legs with my hands cuffed behind me.

Needless to say, my grades turned to shit. And the shit hit the fan when I went home for the holidays that Christmas. My parents thought I must be doing drugs. My mother innocently suggested it might be "girl problems," and I said, "Sure, that's it."

Things started changing again that spring. I was a junior. It was Doug's senior year, and of course I was already wondering what would happen when he graduated. I had no way of knowing that it would all be over before then.

I'd had fantasies before of being made to sexually service him while some of his buddies looked on. One night something like that finally happened. One of Doug's closest buddies, or at least the one he seemed to be spending the most time with that year, was a guy named Gene. Gene was very much in Doug's class, the same caliber, a star athlete with a terrific body as well as good grades and money. He had black hair and looked like he'd just stepped out of an Abercrombie and Fitch ad.

One night Gene dropped over by himself. He and Doug drank beer and talked for a while in the living room. I was in my room, naked, wearing my dog collar. Doug told me to come out. I thought he was kidding, but he'd seen me only a few minutes earlier. He yelled at me again, and this time he said something like, "Get your naked butt out here, cocksucker!"

When I stepped into the room, Gene's eyes were like saucers. Doug pulled out his cock and made me go down on him. From the way Gene talked ("You weren't kidding, he really does it!") I could tell Doug had told him about me and wanted to show me off. After I'd sucked him for a while, he made me suck off Gene. Gene came in my mouth after about two minutes, which was too bad because he had a very nice cock, though nowhere near as nice as Doug's. Then Gene left in a hurry.

But Gene kept coming back. And though the two of them always used me as a bottom, fucking my face and screwing my ass, pretty soon Gene was going down on Doug, and then getting fucked by him. I remember one night, while Doug fucked Gene over the sofa, I groveled behind him and used my mouth on both of them, rimming Doug's ass and rimming Gene's ass as Doug plowed in and out of him, then getting underneath to suck Gene's cock.

Doug started losing interest in me almost immediately. I wasn't really surprised when he started fucking around with Gene, but I was shocked at how quickly he could abandon me. By the end of the term Gene was coming over almost every night, usually sleeping in the bed with Doug, and Doug wasn't even touching me. He hardly even talked to me. It was almost as if the two years had never happened, and we were back to being bare acquaintances who just happened to share an apartment.

At the end of term Doug was very busy finishing up academic requirements and going to graduation parties, usually with Gene, who was also a senior. Once again I was left out. I tried several times to confront him, but we had never really worked out a way of talking and I got nowhere. He no longer had any interest in me sexually or physically, and that was the only way we had ever communicated. I became very quiet and depressed.

Doug had found a position with a company in New York

before he graduated. He was planning on subletting an apartment from a relative, and it seemed like Gene was going to be living with him. I kept asking Doug for the address, and he kept putting me off, until I got the idea he didn't want me to have it. I figured I was only being paranoid, but I was tired of asking so I finally looked through his papers and found it. He packed and left with hardly a good-bye.

I was still obsessed with him. I would lie in bed for hours at night, wearing the collar, masturbating while I remembered all the things he had done to me, all the times he had put his cock in me. I wrote him a few times—not holding back but pouring my heart out—long, pleading, masochistic letters, begging him to use me again. He never answered. I tried to call, but his number was unlisted.

It took me a very long time to get over Doug, at least enough to go out and function on my own. I pulled myself together over the summer and threw myself into studying the next fall, making up for my zombielike performance my junior year. I went out and met other guys, and even found a few boyfriends. Now I'm out of school, and having about as active a sexual and social life as most gay guys my age.

I still dream about finding an experience like the one I had with Doug, but I'm not counting on it, because I don't think I could ever again be so vulnerable and open to such an intense experience, or give myself so unreservedly to another man with no strings attached.

I still beat off thinking about him.

SELF-TAUGHT

Rob Rosen

was majoring in pre-law at a Midwestern liberal arts college.
My classes ran the educational gamut: political science, philosophy, English, nothing I couldn't handle. Still, I had to take at
least one science or math class in order to get my degree. Math
was out; my GPA couldn't tolerate what was sure to be a less
than stellar grade. I opted, instead, for biology. I knew my ass
from my elbow, so I thought I had a fair shot at it. It had been
easy enough in high school, anyway.

Then again, college wasn't high school. And asses and elbows
weren't listed on the syllabus.

Meaning, I was royally fucked, and no lube for miles.

Still, there was one saving grace: Professor Marks may have
been a hard grader, but he was easy on the eyes. Tall, thin,
scruffy, wearing tweed jackets, bow ties, loose-fitting slacks,
horn-rimmed glasses, he was a sexy brainiac. Not that any of
that helped me with my grades, which were lackluster at best,
but at least I had reason to show up for class every day.

Then came midterms and I was fucked again. Hell, I was fisted, still with no lube, not even a gob of spit. My hopes for law school were in danger, my parents way pissed. But there was a saving grace, a glimmer of hope—a fickle finger of fate to loosen me up, two fingers, in fact.

One showed up in the unlikeliest of places: library stacks, archeology section, quiet bathroom. There, a guy could whack his willie in private, in between studying. A guy like me, that is. With one foot on the toilet paper dispenser, legs wide, neck arched down, the tip of my longish cock just making it into my mouth, practice made perfect. See, by my junior year, I could suck myself off, sending a stream of cum down my throat, and making it back to my books in no time flat. A nifty trick, to say the least.

That's how I spotted it, sitting there with my jeans down to the linoleum, my dickhead throbbing in my mouth, close, so fucking close. It was in black ink: *Mister Marks trades blow jobs*. I shot a hefty load just thinking about it, a trickle of spunk gliding down my chin.

"Huh," I whispered. "What's he trade 'em for?"

And that second fated finger? Well, turned out, Mister Marks kept after-hours, tutoring. You just had to sign up and show up, twenty minutes per student. By then, I needed the help, desperately. But how does a student broach the subject of trading blow jobs without getting expelled—or having his butt kicked? Or both?

I guessed I'd have to play that one by ear.

I signed up, showing up in his office at seven, the last after-hours slot. The walls were covered in diplomas, no family snapshots. That was a good sign. Marks showed up. He was dressed casually in jeans, a button-down, short sleeves revealing hairy forearms and sinew. He smiled, got right down to business. We sat with books open, no small talk, him across from me barely catching my eye, try as I might. The guy had stellar eyes, too, strikingly blue, dazzling under the fluorescent lighting. In truth, the one-on-one studying was helpful, though it did little for my throbbing cock.

Still, I'd get my chance.

It was two weeks until my finals. I'd had two months of tutoring. My grades had climbed. I just needed a little boost now. Time for a trade?

"You're doing much better, Mr. Peters," he commented at the end of our last session. He smiled, his teeth white, even. The dude obviously had a good orthodontist as a kid.

"Thanks to you," I replied.

He shrugged, reached for his jacket. "I like my students to succeed."

The way he said succeed, emphasis on the *suck*, sent my mind spinning. Yeah, I was grasping at straws. Still, it was worth it to go for broke. We'd become, if not friends, then at least friendly. "Um, I thought you should know, I saw, well, some derogatory comments about you in a bathroom in the library." I paused, swallowed hard. "I, um, scratched them out."

Then he paused, turning my way, jacket in hand. "Students can be cruel," he replied, his eyes suddenly on mine, drilling down deep. "What, um, what did it say?"

I coughed, my nerves suddenly leaving me, legs trembling a bit. "Oh, nothing really. Never mind. I just, just wanted to repay you for, well, you know." Still, I wasn't dumb. If he could emphasize the *suck*, I could emphasize the *repay*.

We stood there like that, his small office seemingly growing smaller, the air suddenly hot, the sound of our breathing getting louder. "Thank you, Mr. Peters."

He nodded, slightly, his eyes remaining on mine. "Still, I'm curious what my students have to say about me."

Was he baiting me, or, as he said, just curious? In any case, my answering him now wouldn't end up with that kicked ass. I looked down, focusing on his brown penny loafers. "It, um, said, *Mister Marks trades blow jobs*." The last word came out sotto voce.

He chuckled. "What do I trade them for?"

I looked back up, echoing his laughter with my own. "I asked myself the exact same thing."

He paused again, the stare continuing, scrutinizing me while a lemon-sized pit formed in my stomach. "And what did you come up with?"

Emphasis on the *come*. Not imagined this time. His voice was tinged with something now, a nervousness, an edge. "Better grades, I'd imagine, sir," I replied. This time, I stared back at him, eye to eye, muddy brown on dazzling blue.

He laughed again shortly. "That would have to be one hell of a blow job, Mr. Peters."

My head began to swim, the sound of his wall clock nearly deafening. "Guess so," I replied, a spasm to my smile, a lone bead of sweat forming on my brow. "Too bad."

Then, quick as a wink, "Too bad, what? That I don't, or you don't?"

I sat back down, the terror forming in my chest almost unbearable. "Oh, I, um, I've never, well, given one." And then, strangely, I relaxed, regrouped. "I mean, to anyone other than myself."

He returned his jacket to the rack. Bing-fucking-o. "To yourself?"

I blushed, a flash of crimson spreading across my cheeks. "Sure. Not too difficult."

"Trust me, Mr. Peters, if such was the case, every man would be doing it. And bragging about it."

Again I looked up at him, my knees bouncing in place, my voice catching in my throat. "You've never tried to, well...you know?"

He scratched his head, clearly thinking of his next move. This was difficult ground; he had to tread lightly. "Maybe in my younger days. Just to see if I could."

"And?"

His smile returned, big and bright and glorious. "Not even close."

I laughed. "Just takes some practice." Hesitating, holding my knees still, I added, "I could, um, show you how. I mean, look at all you've taught me; it's the least I can do."

He shook his head, curly hair, shoulder length, moving from side to side. "That wouldn't be appropriate, Mr. Peters."

I stood, now an inch in front of him. "Yeah, you're right, sir. Sorry." I moved to the door, my hand reaching out, not inadvertently brushing the front of his jeans, the bulge obvious. I glanced back up. "You could just watch, though. No trading. Nothing wrong with that. A teaching thing."

His breathing became erratic. He blinked, once, twice. Then came a short raspy, "Okay."

"Okay?"

"Something new." He nodded. "Fine, let's see this *talent* of yours, Mr. Peters."

Again I reached for the doorknob, but only to lock it. Then I moved away, a space of about two feet forming between us, enough for him to watch and for me to undress. I kicked off my sneakers, placing them neatly by the door, joining them with my socks. He watched, in silence. I continued, also without a word, yanking my T-shirt out of my jeans and then off, folding it and placing it atop my shoes and socks. I moved methodically, clinically, my heart pounding. The belt was unbuckled, the jeans slid down, off, folded as well. Then it was just me and my boxers, the tenting noticeable. He stood there, arms akimbo, waiting for the crescendo. I nodded, gulped, and slid down my underwear, my cock springing out, swaying as I set the final article on the floor.

I sat in the chair staring up at him, naked, rigid. I started to speak, the words getting stuck, then began again. "I, um, need to put a foot up on your desk, sir."

"Oh, sure," he managed.

I raised my foot, my legs splaying far apart, and craned my neck down, the leaking helmeted head just a fraction of an inch away. "See, I can get the tip in, sir. Gotta strain my back, but…" And then I was sucking the head, a jolt of adrenalin shooting down my spine and up through my still-thickening cock. I stared at him while sucking away. He stared down in rapt attention.

"That as far you can go, Mr. Peters?"

I popped it out. "Like I said, just the head, sir." I laughed. "Still, it seems to do the trick."

He moved to my side, his hand suddenly on my upper back. "Mind if I, um, help? Push you down a bit?"

A novel approach. I liked the sound of it. "Please. That would be, um, awesome."

And, like he said, it helped. A great deal. His pushing was all I needed, my one inch of downed flesh quickly becoming two, three, my mouth bobbing up and down on my granite-hard prick, sucking the length of it, my eyes fluttering in newfound ecstasy.

He eased up, my cock popping out. "Thanks," I said. "See, that's why you're the teacher, sir."

He grinned, moving back to a couple of feet in front of me. "You're welcome. And you're a good student."

I sat back up, my dick pointing at him. I clenched, made it

bob. "But I could, I could, um, show you how, though. The student becomes the teacher." Now it was my turn to emphasize the word *come*.

He sighed, scratched his chin, smiled wider. I supposed since I was already naked and hard in his office, he had little left to lose. He kicked off his shoes with a nod. "Okay, Mr. Peters." I sat and watched, my throat suddenly dry, my own breathing now irregular, my cock coursing with blood. He rolled down his socks, unhooked his tie, and placed them both next to my stuff. Slowly, he unbuttoned his shirt, a matting of chest hair suddenly revealed, trailing down to a flat belly, rife with dense muscle, two hard pink nipples. He looked up, still smiling, noticed my ogling and leering. "Yoga. Keeps me in shape." He patted his stomach as he set his shirt down.

"Should make our, um, *session* easier. You being bendy, and all," I commented.

He snickered, reaching for his belt, unbuckling it before flipping open his jeans and sliding down his zipper. Then he was standing before me in nothing but a pair of tenting boxers. And then not even those. My eyes roamed up and down his lean body, hairy jogger's legs, heavy balls swaying as he set his boxers down, a thick prick, seven hard inches, curved to the side, veined, a wiry bush, jet black.

"Um, ready," he announced, pointing down to his raging boner.

"Um, yeah, I can see that," I replied, standing up to offer him my seat. He walked by, his hand brushing my cock. I jumped, groaned. "Sorry."

He ignored the remark and sat down, staring up at me. "Now what, Mr. Peters?"

"Um, try doing what I did, sir. Put a foot on your desk. Let's see how close you can get your mouth to your, um, your dick."

We were two naked hard men, alone, and, yes, I found it difficult to speak that way in front of him. Still, I persevered. And,
of course, I gently stroked my cock all the while. He did as I
asked, his legs suddenly far apart, his pink crinkled hole in view,
a whirl of hair surrounding it, balls hanging low, cock pointing
up. Dude was a sight to see—best biology lesson I ever had.

Still, his mouth was a good several inches away from where it
needed to be, try as he might to get it there. I walked over, placing
my hand on his back, as he had done for me. At the touch of
flesh on flesh a spark traveled from him to me before eddying
joyously around my stomach. I pushed down. He grunted, his
tongue darting out. Close, but no cigar.

"This way isn't going to work," I eventually told him.

"Any other ideas, Mr. Peters?" He looked up, still smiling.
Guy was enjoying this, no doubt about it.

I moved back in front of him, squinting my eyes in thought.
"Try putting your feet back on the floor and grabbing the bottom
of the seat. That should give you some leverage while you're
craning your neck." This got him closer to his goal, but with his
hard cock against his belly and his hands now busy, he wasn't in
the right sucking position.

I crouched in front of him, placing my hand on the back of
his neck as I shoved downward. Again he grunted. Closer than
before. Almost there. "Um, mind if I hold it for you, sir?" I
asked, timidly, excitedly, eager to grab hold of his fat cock.

We were now eye to eye, him in the chair, me in front, one
hand still on his neck, the other finally gripping his prick, holding
it just beneath his mouth, feeling it pulse, widen in my hand. He
moaned upon contact, still trying to get his mouth around it.

A final push and we were there, his lips sucking the tip,
licking the precum off. It was beautiful to witness so up close and
personal like; too beautiful, in fact, to not participate. I moved

his prick away from his mouth and leaned in. He watched me, silently, as I mirrored his actions, licking the tip, sucking the head, then handing it back to him to do the same. Back and forth it went, soon slick with spit, the room filling with the sound of his moans each time I'd suck and lick and gulp down on his rod. And then, at last, we met in the middle, both of us sucking the head, our lips colliding, soft as down.

"Um, Mr. Peters," he eventually said.

"Yes, Mr. Marks?" I replied, his cock now between us, my hand slowly jerking it.

He chuckled. "I think my neck and back are about to give out. Mind if we try a new position?"

I moved away, standing back up. "What do you have in mind, sir?" I asked, my voice gravelly, enthusiastic for anything he now had in store for us, the teacher, apparently, back to his teaching ways.

He grabbed his coat and placed it against a wall. Soon enough, his neck and shoulders were on top of it, his back flush against the wall, his legs hanging over, apart, dick dangling down. I knew my role in this. I walked in, my body pressing down on his feet, pushing his cock low, lower still, near his opened mouth. I had a super view of his ass now. I ran my hands across each alabaster cheek, down the hair-lined crack, my fingers swirling around his twitching hole.

When I could hear him sucking the tip of his dick, I leaned in for a whiff, the smell of musk and sweat invading my sinus cavity. I took a cursory lick around the ring, zooming in to the winking center, diving my tongue inside. He grounded loudly while I reamed him out, parting him for better access, filling his chute with my slithering appendage.

He popped his prick out of his mouth. "That feels good, Mr. Peters."

But I had one more trick up my sleeve—or up his ass, as was the case. I got on my knees, again taking his cock from him for a suck, my free hand roaming his butt until it found the sweet spot, a lone index finger gliding in and up and back, soon joined by its shorter neighbor, nothing fickle or fated about them. I placed his dick back in his mouth for him, jerking my own cock while he sucked himself off and I fucked his ass silly with my digits, his moans now loud if not muffled, mine gaining momentum as we both coaxed the cum from our balls.

With my fingers now entrenched up his ass, ramming up against his stone-solid prostate, I knew we didn't have long. I sped up the pace on my cock and his hole. Seconds later, he groaned, long and low and deep, his back and legs quaking as he shot his load down his throat, much of it spilling out and over, dripping across his face. My cock exploded a split second later, dousing the floor with ounce after sticky ounce of molten-hot cum, my body spasming, my head jerked back, mouth open, a raspy exhale released.

He tumbled over, panting, flat on the floor. I stared down at him, all hair and muscle, his face sticky and white, his cock still hard, dribbling. "That is a useful talent, Mr. Peters," he managed, gulping to catch his breath.

"Yes, sir," I replied. "Comes in, um, handy."

He laughed and rolled over, watching me as I got dressed. "Good luck on your final," he eventually said as I reached for the knob, opening the door. "But you'll have to earn whatever grade you get; I don't trade blow jobs for that."

I echoed his laugh as I stared down at him. "What *do* you trade them for, sir?"

He sat back up, Indian-style. "Why, for other blow jobs, of course, Mr. Peters. Looks like I owe you one."

I smiled, nodded, and exited his office, closing the door behind me, though not for the last time. Not by a long shot. Thankfully, I aced the test and the class, the exam counting for a whopping 60 percent of my final grade. But, like he said, he owed me one. And I eagerly cashed in on that promise, repeatedly, teacher becoming student, student becoming teacher. Emphasis on the *come*—ample, throat-soaking quantities of it.

THE SILENT HUSTLER

Sean Meriwether

Are You a Gay Virgin?
Write about your first anal experience with another man for a private collector. Payment based on the quality and uniqueness of the story. By appointment only.

College can cost you, especially when you have to foot the bill on your own with only a little assistance from the state. I had to hustle up odd jobs to generate income since I didn't have enough experience to score a part-time gig in New York. When I read the ad in the *Village Voice*, I hoped my virginity would pay off.

I dialed the number from the ad, repeating the dialogue I'd scripted in my head beforehand. *Keep your voice low and sound professional*, I coached.

A baritone greeted me. "Hello?"

I fumbled with the phone, my script forgotten immediately.

I almost hung up. "Uh...I'm calling about the ad in the *Voice*; I'm a...virgin and I uh..." A flush ran over me choking off the words.

"Hold the line." Silence followed.

I caught my breath and waited for the man to return. Instead, asthmatic breathing filled my ear, followed by a voice that seemed to belong to a heavy and thick-jowled man. "To whom am I speaking?"

"Who, me?"

"You phoned about the ad. May I have your name, son?"

I blanked, not wanting to give my real one. I spotted loose change on the table, all I had to my name for the rest of the week. "Abraham." I stopped myself from adding Lincoln.

"Thank you, *Abraham*. May I first confirm that you are a virgin? By virgin I mean that you have not engaged in anal sex."

I juggled my past history of backseat blow jobs and front-seat hand jobs. "No, not that."

"Your age?"

"Twenty-one."

"What school are you attending?"

"What?"

"I presume you are in college. Is this not the case?"

"Yeah."

"Have you written work of an erotic nature previously?"

"Sorta."

"Have you published any work to date?"

"Yeah."

"May I ask what you have published?"

"You know, stuff."

"Would you like to be anally penetrated?"

My eyes searched the dusty plain beneath my dorm mate's

bed; a tied-off condom filled with Joe's spunk. *Yes, I'd like to get fucked.*

"The purpose of this exercise is to document your first anal experience. If you are not interested in having one this conversation is moot."

"Yes, sir."

"Yes, sir, what?"

"Yes, sir. I would like to…have an anal experience."

"Good. Good. You shall come see me. Bring a sample of your writing and I will negotiate our terms at that time."

I scribbled down the address on the inside cover of my human sexuality textbook, somewhat fearful that this heavy breathing pervert was going to be doing the penetrating.

I arrived a few minutes late, having rushed from the A train. The doorman stopped me at the front desk and asked my name, but I couldn't remember which president I'd used as an alias. "Is it Thomas? Or George? Try Abraham."

The doorman nodded severely. "Seventh floor. Mr. Y. has been expecting you." He directed me to the elevator, an Art Deco affair that made me long for the streamlined future of the distant past.

The elevator opened onto a vestibule where a broad-shouldered man greeted me. His eyes were angelic blue, cut from the sky. "This way." I followed him through towering stacks of boxes, books and furniture. The path led to a larger room filled with a mind-numbing number of possessions. In the center of this white elephant sale sat a massive man in a larger chair; a replica of my escort stood behind him. The angel-eyed man offered me the sofa opposite the heavy breather, then joined his twin to flank the old man. I pushed aside antique copies of the *Advocate* and perched on the edge.

"So." Mr. Y. laced his fingers to create a bridge, rested his massive head upon it. His lips pursed, as if he were trying to determine the fates of millions.

"So." I mirrored his posture without intending parody.

"Tell me about yourself, *Abraham*." His upward inflection confirmed that he knew my name was a lie, but would entertain me for the moment.

I raced to explain myself. "I'm in college, just started, right? Fresh meat. Putting myself through and all. Doing this and that, odd jobs, to pay for books and the like. Right? I grew up in New Jersey and..."

"And you'll admit it," one of the angelic men snickered.

I flushed and changed course. "I've always written and I haven't like done *it* or anything, so when I saw your ad, I thought I could use the money. I mean...wow, I'm nervous." I wiped sweaty palms along my legs.

"Point one," the man raised a chubby finger. "Remove extraneous verbiage from your dialogue."

"What do you mean?

"Do not waste my time with information that does not advance your story." He rebridged his hands and leaned forward, the moon of his face on a crash course with mine. "You are attractive enough. I am certain you will be successful in your pursuit of intercourse. Frankly, I am surprised that you have not already succeeded in that endeavor. Please tell me, *Abraham*, why is this?"

"What do you mean?" I looked at the two beautiful men flanking the ogre.

"He asked why no one has already popped your cherry," one of the men joked. They both laughed.

I stared at the floor littered with newspapers.

"Gentlemen, please excuse us for the duration of our conversation." I watched the two men retreat to the kitchen, where the swinging door concealed them but I was sure they continued to listen and make fun of me.

"How many men have you been with?"

"Twelve," I said, but that number had nothing to do with me. This was how many men my dorm mate, Joe, was seeing...this month. I didn't know how he had the time to attend class.

"None of them entertained the notion of penetration?"

"None of them succeeded."

"Do you read?"

"I love to read. I'm an English major and..."

"Are you familiar with the work of Anaïs Nin?"

"Yeah, sure."

"Have you read this?" He indicated a volume on the table between us. "I suggest you read this before you begin your enterprise." I picked up a thumbed paperback of *Delta of Venus*. "You may keep it. I have many copies."

I flipped through it quickly, as if I'd read it a dozen times. "Sure."

"Please say yes when you mean yes."

I nodded. "Yes, sir."

"May I have your sample?"

"Excuse me?"

"Your writing sample, I believe it was a requirement we discussed over the phone."

"Yeah, right." I fumbled it out of my back pocket, flattened the few sheets I'd printed and offered it to him.

"I see how important the presentation of your work is to you." He took the butt-wrinkled pages, exhaled laboriously and settled back in his chair. His eyes descended to the page and he lost himself in the text. I took the opportunity to review the surroundings, the jumble of objects, the landslide of possessions. *How could anyone live like this?*

He finished too quickly. "Your prose has a unique, shall we say, *rawness*, but as with your person and grammar it lacks structure and discipline. You can not hang a story on a few nicely turned phrases."

I flushed, irritated by his critique. I was more accustomed to the negligible comments from workshop peers who wanted you to parrot nice things about their own stories.

"Now, we shall negotiate payment. Based on your sample I am prepared to offer you $500 for a ten-thousand word piece about your first anal experience."

Dollar bills danced before my eyes. I'd never had five hundred dollars all at once. I'd roll around in it naked and giggle...but the cautionary side of me took a step back. "What if I can't write that much? That's like one hundred pages. What if I can only write five thousand words, would you still pay me?"

"It is only forty double-spaced pages, *Abraham*. Depending on the quality of the work I might pay you a lesser amount."

"What if it's only two thousand words, like that story I gave you. What would you pay me for that?"

"I may still pay you, but I would not agree to a figure until after I have read it."

"Please don't be angry, but what about five hundred words, would you accept that?"

"For that I have no use." He sat back, enthroned in his massive chair.

"Can I ask what you get out of this?"

A mysterious smile framed his lips, one that made Mona Lisa's transparent. "I am a collector, as you may have noted. I have my reasons for collecting stories where men bare their bodies and souls on the page. My only requirement is that you provide me with the only copy, written out legibly in long hand. I shall be the sole owner."

"How would you know if I kept a copy?"

"This is my only stipulation for payment and is not negotiable. You are writing this story for me and me alone."

"Sure, right." His mouth turned down and I quickly corrected myself with, "Yes, sir."

"Return to me in a week's time. I want the whole experience, the connection with another male, the details of the moment of penetration, the perception of your body and your mental state. These are important elements that must be captured."

"And if I can't get anyone to, uh, participate inside a week?"

"That is not my concern. Please take the book and read it. I will see you this time next week."

"Yeah, okay…yes, sir." The angelic man was only too eager to show me out.

I lay on my bed, head dangling over the edge, watching Joe do push-ups upside down. He was shirtless and his lean torso lifted and dropped with mechanical precision. I imagined being under him, naked, then writing about it.

"Joe, how do get a guy into bed?"

He paused, arms stretched, sweat drawing a line down the seat of his gray shorts, parting the heavens.

"Blokes are easy. You just tell them what they want and they go along happily." He returned to his workout, a daily routine I made sure not to miss.

"Yeah, but…"

"You're a lovely lad, Puppy, but you should be out there doing it instead of chatting me up." He rolled onto his back, started doing sit-ups.

"Well, maybe I need someone to, you know, walk me through it. Someone I trusted." I took a deep breath, the smell of his sweat and dirty socks mixing up my thoughts. "Like you, maybe."

He gave a bark of a laugh as he sat up and looked hard at me. "Do it with *you*? You're like my baby brother, Ryan." A huge smile lit his face. "Oh, you're having me on, aren't you?"

"Yeah," I said, deflated, defeated. I watched him continue torturing his body into perfection. I ran my hand over my own sparrow chest, concave stomach. I was too skinny; no one would ever want me. Five hundred dollars can-canned out of my reach.

"Do you know anyone who would be, I don't know, interested in fucking me?"

"What?"

"I mean, like one of your boyfriends. How many do you need, anyways?"

"I wouldn't set you up with any of those cottagers. They're single use only. What you want is a boyfriend."

"I don't want a *boyfriend*. I *need* to get *laid*." I sat up on my bed, tilted my head to the right, then the left, changing my perspective of Joe. "Look, you'd be doing me a favor. I mean, you've done it with all these other guys, what's one more? We could do it right now, if you're free."

Joe continued with his crunches. "You're desperate. They smell it. On you. Scares them." He stood up and started working with free weights, sweaty muscles in motion.

I buried my face under the pillow and drilled my eyes into the naked wall, seeing nothing but sweaty Joes.

"Let's pop out for a drink, then. We'll tag team a couple of blokes."

"No," I said, mouth full of pillow. "I have a paper to finish."

"Don't shit on me for the truth, Puppy."

I listened to him grunt through the rest of his workout, then strip down and step into the shower. The worst part of college was having a queer roommate who was a flagrant exhibitionist. I never wanted to leave our room for fear I'd miss one second of his performance. However, his blunt advice and lack of interest in sex with me kept me facing the wall. I'd spent years in high school servicing nervous married men and fellow students who would torment me in school the next day. Escaping to New York was supposed to be a cure for that rural existence, not a continuation of the curse. I'd die a virgin, a penniless one.

Joe stepped out of the shower, his wet feet padding across the floor. I turned my head and watched him cross the room, the twin moons of his ass floating above strong legs. Martyrs suffered less torture. "I'll come."

"Where?" Joe turned around, exposing the front half of him. I sat up to get a better view.

"Out for a drink." I smiled, throat painfully dry.

"You sure?"

"I'm not as innocent as you think."

"Never said you were innocent, love, just naïve. You're a puppy looking for his master." Joe stepped into a tight pair of briefs, arranged his package for symmetry.

"I'm older than you so stop calling me Puppy."

"No offense."

"I could screw around with a bunch of guys like you. I'm a writer. I need to experience life to write about it."

"Yeah, but you wouldn't enjoy it. It's not what you're about. You're all flowers and romance. You lap up that treacle, love, but it's what gets you off." He laughed gently, stopped by my bed on his way to the closet, ruffled my hair. "Get ready, mate, we'll do an East Village bar crawl. Find you a fuck buddy worthy of your Puppiness."

I panted like a real puppy, playfully dug my head into the meat of Joe's hand. Licked it.

"Good dog."

We'd had no success by the third bar. I'd rejected the handful of guys who showed the least bit of interest, comparing them with Joe and finding them sorely inadequate. Joe impatiently upped the ante. "Let's head to Lot's Wife. They have a back room and the best salted margaritas in the free world. We'll find a bedmate for you there. Or at least something for your big brother."

Joe led us past the line waiting to get in, smiled at the man on the door. He was greeted with a bear hug and a soft kiss. "Howdy, Joe."

"What's it like tonight?"

"Wall of flesh in there. Why don't you angels stay out here and keep me company?"

"Sorry, love, we can't dally. Lover boy here needs a cock up his arse."

I flushed and tried to fade into the pavement, but the bald-headed guy had already dismissed me. "No minnows for me, you know I like my men with some meat on their bones." His hand groped Joe's cock; I flushed with jealousy.

"Your virginal daughters, too," Joe snarked.

Joe grabbed my hand and led me inside. We were bathed in human humidity, joining us to the Hydra-headed man-fest, a pumping, jumping display of body parts moving to the pounding music. Joe guided me around the crowd to the bar. He ordered a round and for the fourth time of the evening, didn't need to pay.

We sipped margaritas and searched the club with our eyes. Men danced naked, made out, and one couple on stage mimicked sex, or was it an act? Hands reached out from the dark and stroked their wet skin. I drank quickly.

"How about that one?" Joe's hot breath was in my ear. He

pointed out a short, stocky blond with art school chin beard, the complete opposite of Joe.

"No way." I took the opportunity to study the side of Joe's face, the scruff of his sideburn, the shell of his ear.

"What the fuck are you looking for?"

"Someone interesting."

"Jesus, lad, you aren't going to talk to them. You fuck them and go home."

I nodded, the tequila working into my bloodstream to join the beer, rum and vodka from the previous bars. I tried to climb up on the stool to scan the crowd, but Joe tugged me down by my belt loops. "Don't be so eager, Puppy. You'll frighten them off. Blokes are like sheep; you need to be careful not to startle them."

I nodded and looked around, finding each boy beautiful in a generic way, but none of them Joe. I knew I was keeping him from his normal evening out and the idea of ruining his chances for his *boy de nuit* made me ready to call it a night. "I'll go back to the dorm, you stay."

"We came together, we'll leave together." Joe ordered another round. "After one more."

"Okay." I watched Joe search the crowd, followed his gaze to a boy who emerged from the throng. He wasn't exactly another Joe, but there was a resemblance. He weaved his way to the bar, empty glass in hand.

I pointed him out to Joe. "How about that one."

Joe smiled. "You're reading my mind."

I reached out and stopped the boy. He smiled at me, I smiled at Joe.

"Hey, little dude." No accent, no perfect body, no spiky hair or endearingly crooked smile, but almost like Joe. The boy wobbled, dropped his glass short of the bar. Joe's breath was back against the side of my face. "He's drunk. Let's take him home. We can share." He reached around me and placed a salted margarita in the boy's hand. "On the house, love."

The boy nodded and smiled, head bobbing off beat from the music. Joe maneuvered himself around me to the boy's side, nuzzled his mouth up against his ear. The boy drank while he listened, eyebrows puzzled up, then his eyes flashed at me. "Him?" He pointed at me with a half-empty glass. Joe was back at his ear as the boy polished off his drink. They turned around and moved to the door, me, as always, bringing up the rear.

I joined them on the sidewalk. The new boy stood to the side of the entrance, fumbling with a cigarette. Joe lit it for him and the drunken boy smiled. "You're so cute." His exaggerated gesture would have been as admissible as a breathalyzer test.

I pulled Joe to the side. "Is this a good idea?"

"Best of the evening. He's not bad. Kind of fancy him myself."

"Yeah, sure, he looks like you, but he's wasted."

"So are you."

The night swam in circles around me and I latched on to Joe for anchorage. He draped his arm around my shoulders, maneuvered me forward. "Don't turn around, just walk and wait." We marched a few steps, the sidewalk hard to navigate with lighter than average feet, while the club evaporated into the night behind us. "Dudes. Where you going?"

"Don't stop." Joe pushed me forward, closing in on the curb. We stopped at the light and the boy caught up with us.

"Back to yours?" Joe asked without turning around.

"Fuck, yeah."

Joe whispered in my ear. "See, Puppy. All you need to do is tell them what they want and they always come around."

We pounded down a flight of stairs to the boy's basement

apartment. The Pullman kitchen was in a closet off the room, littered with dishes, two mattresses lay parallel on the floor. Clothing and books were stacked in milk crates. The tiny window made the room feel like a cave.

"First things first, *dude*." Joe pinned the boy against the wall, jailed him with his body. "You clean? Any STDs we need to know about? HIV positive?" He leaned in and kissed the side of the boy's face. "Don't lie. I'll know if you're lying."

"Shit, no, dude. I'm clean. Really. I don't, you know…with a roommate and all. He's straight. But home. For the weekend."

"Good." Joe released the boy and steered him to the first mattress.

"That's his," he said.

"It doesn't matter."

"Okay." The boy sat down heavily, took off his shoes and socks. Fumbled with his pants.

I pleaded with Joe. "I'm not sure this is a good idea."

"Isn't this what we came for?"

"Isn't this a little weird with your brother and all?"

"He's shy. Needs big brother's minding to get him humped."

"I'd be totally freaked watching my brother get fucked."

"You told him I'm your brother?"

"Does it matter to you, *dude*?"

"No…yeah. It's sorta hot. Are you gonna join in?"

Joe clapped his hands on my shoulder. "Let's get naked, gentlemen."

The boy struggled to remove his jeans and briefs. Naked he looked even less like Joe, but in the dim light it was enough to pretend. I took off my shirt, removed my shoes one at a time, and took off my pants with painstaking precision. I sat down next to the guy, arms crossed over my small chest.

"Geez, you're so skinny. That's way hot."

"Yeah?"

"I like guys who are smaller than me."

"Yeah?"

"Ryan, why don't you kiss him," Joe directed from the adjacent bed. The boy leaned in clumsily, his mouth hard against mine, the sooty taste of ash on his tongue. He leaned me over and we collapsed onto the bed. His hands, mouth and cock seemed to be everywhere at once, so unlike the boys who only let me blow them. My body went into sensory overload and froze.

"You okay, Ryan?"

I nodded as the boy's head traveled south, his mouth on my cock in my underwear, than out of it. I watched Joe watch us, waiting for him to join. I groaned, getting too close too quickly. Joe clapped his hands together. "Let's take this up a notch." He tossed over a condom and a small packet of lube. "Who does who?"

"I uh, I'll go first." I rolled over on my stomach and pulled down my underwear in the back. I turned my head and stared at Joe in the dark, hoping this was getting him hard.

"Be careful with my Puppy," Joe said to the boy, who was fumbling with the condom. Cool jelly spilled between my buttcheeks, then the weight of another body was upon me, pushing me into the dirty sheets. The boy poked aimlessly, just missing the spot, then zeroed in and inched forward. He groaned as he went in. It hurt at first, and I tried to inch away, but Joe told me to relax and I stopped clenching down. A fullness spread up into me, burned. The boy pumped once, twice, three times and collapsed on me with a groan. "Oh, shit." It was over.

I looked at Joe, a shifting pattern of darkness refusing to take shape. He stood up, tugged his shirt over his head to bare his perfect stomach, and dropped his pants to expose the erection I'd been waiting for. He approached the bed and tapped my arm. "Go sit over there, Puppy."

I disengaged myself and moved to the other bed. Joe slicked his dick up with spit, then rolled a condom on and lubed himself up with one hand. He dropped on top of the boy with no preliminaries, arranged the kid's legs to suit himself and then plunged ahead. The boy tried to squirm away at first, then gave up with an aching exhalation, "Oh, man."

Joe fucked him just like his workout, a metronomic pounding. Their fucking was marked only by the boy's soft moan each time Joe thrust in, each stroke marking two-second intervals. A minute became five, ten, eternity, while I sat mesmerized by the rise and fall of my roommate's ass. Joe picked up the pace, pounded the boy into the mattress—the boy cried out to god. Joe came with a grunt, his face twisted and alien. He kneeled, pulled the condom off and dropped it between the boy's splayed legs. "Get dressed, Puppy. We're done."

"Wow. That was…" the boy rolled over, hand on his cock, jerking himself off. "Dude, that was awesome."

Joe pulled on his briefs, pants and shirt before I had a chance to locate my clothes. I looked down at the boy as he masturbated, their sex thick in my nose, angered that it wasn't me Joe'd fucked and never would be.

Joe was at the door before I had my shoes on. "Call me, dude. Like, for real." Joe didn't look back, just opened the door and left. I rushed into my clothes and tossed a hasty apology to the boy on the bed before running out to catch up with Joe; he quickened his pace when I joined him. Silent cabs sailed up 4th Avenue, circling the sleeping city.

"Get what you wanted?"

"No."

"Didn't think so. He was a terrible lay."

"He seemed to enjoy you."

"No resistance. They need to fight back a little."

"I don't understand."

"You wouldn't, it's not your scene, but you're so damned stupid that you'll just give it away to shits like that. You deserve better than arseholes like me. I'll only fuck you over, Puppy. Time you moved on."

I stopped cold, the memory of him dropping the used condom flaring up in me. I had no idea who this man was; his retreating form belonged to a stranger. I spun around and walked the opposite direction, certain that he wouldn't notice or care that I was gone. He didn't call after me, didn't disrupt the surreal calm of 4:00 a.m. to apologize for making me watch him fuck some guy whose name I didn't even know, rejecting me every step of the way.

I ran back to the boy's apartment. The door was unlocked and I let myself in without knocking. I took off my clothes as he asked, "Where's your brother?" I didn't answer, only lay down next to him and let him do what he wanted, using his clumsy hands to erase any trace of Joe from my memory.

"I want to note my displeasure at being mentioned in your story. That is not what this exercise was about." Mr. Y. looked up from the composition notebook that was filled end to end with his commission. He'd been reading straight through for the last forty minutes while I ticked off the time, eager for payment.

"You set the ball in motion." I tried to suppress a yawn. I'd been living at the library the entire week, daring to go back to the dorm only when I knew Joe was going to be out. I couldn't face him, not yet. I only wanted to get the whole experience behind me.

"What of your brother now? What of dearest Rob?"

"He fucks me every morning before class."

"It's very engaging to read such love in your words. You

obviously care for this fellow. The incest does not bother you?"

"My only regret is that we didn't start sooner." He believed it, confirmation that I was a good author. I'd blended my adoration of Joe with my past fumbling experiences, the other boys I'd fallen mistakenly in love with, and topped it off with that moment of penetration to keep it authentic. I'd woven strips of life into a reality where my husband could be my roommate, brother and symbiotic lover. "We're in love, but our parents must never know."

"This is, shall we say, a very personal journey. It's a shame you have to turn it over to me instead of your brother."

I flipped him my smile, perfected by lying to myself. "He's got the real thing. Those are just words on a page."

"True, true. While there is a certain roughness in areas, overall it will be a welcome addition to my collection." He handed the composition notebook to one of the angelic men, then patted the other's arm with his chubby hand. He held up one finger. The second twin quizzed him silently, then shrugged. He navigated the detritus and handed me a sealed envelope. "I trust that will complete our arrangement," Mr. Y. said. I watched the angelic men retreat with my notebook, never to be seen by my eyes again.

"I would appreciate it if you kept me apprised of your publications, son. If this mundane exercise can elicit such tales of love and valor, I imagine you have bigger things in store."

"It was not an easy thing to admit...on the page."

"I am sure it was no easy task."

The image of Joe dropping the condom on the bed returned; he would always be that man to me now, eternally stepping away from the just-fucked boy left behind. I pocketed the envelope and stood, hoping it would be enough to help me find another roommate, at least until the semester ended. The heavy man extended his hand and I took it, looking away from his gaze, staring instead at the littered floor.

"May I ask your real name?"

"It's Joe. Joe McCarthy."

"The same as the man who created the blacklist? You jest, son."

"My parents are English. They didn't know anything until we moved here and then the damage was already done."

"Ah, the story only gets more interesting. Please stay in touch, Mr. McCarthy."

"Yes, sir." I had it down cold.

"Good boy," he said, harking back to "Good dog," Joe's last official words to me before everything changed. I was still the same, but everything else was different.

I turned around in the mess of his apartment and walked along the path through the mountains of boxes and let myself out. I did not check the envelope until I was safely within the wooden confines of the elevator, where I counted out one thousand dollars. I wanted to spend it as quickly as it had come, put the whole experience in the past; it had already cost too much.

DORM

Tom Cardamone

I want a boyfriend who smokes.

None of these boys smoke. Freshman year algebra, I sit in the back of the class and think about leaving during the break. The boys sitting in front of me are all obscenely healthy, all have roughly the same haircut, wear the same T-shirts emblazoned with the scrawled monikers of similar bands and they all like the one girl in class, the prettiest, who won't date any of them. I wouldn't date them either, they move in packs and leave the same smell whenever too many of them are in the same room without decent ventilation: a broth of meaty breath and fresh deodorant.

Leaving during the break I walk off campus and down Main Street. Our school is a not-so-ancient institution trying to look ancient via jumbles of ivory and faux-gothic architecture. Town is a few blocks away and consists of only a few blocks itself. The old movie theater and the courthouse and the church are the only buildings on Main Street over two stories tall. Two movies are playing at the lone theater, some classic film from the thirties and a new horror movie. I don't like black-and-white films. They shouldn't be called black-and-white films; they're gray, gray as worn highways. My favorite movie as a child was *Day of the Triffids*, where giant plants start growing all over the earth, wildly, rapidly expanding, filling cities, killing everyone. Everyone's been struck blind by a meteor, a supernova, something too bright, I forget what. I particularly liked a blind couple who pretended to have sight, to get help from some of the people who could still see. They were blind for so long they knew how to act like they could see. When I was really young I thought the black-and-white films on television were completely accurate: the world used to be gray, color exploding sometime in the sixties I imagined, shooting through the world like Triffids, killing the Eliot Ness my father adored, drowning whole genres (though some shows survived the flood, "Lost in Space," "I Dream of Jeannie," making it to shore soaked in bright shades of Technicolor, anything on horseback perished) erasing a world of fedoras and Buicks, flooding television with every hue, blinding some, hypnotizing others.

Though I want a boyfriend I have never actually kissed another boy. I've thought about it, but which boy? The boys at the dorm are either dull or madly animal, boys following any hunger or thirst to its brutal conclusion. I've never kissed a boy but I've kissed myself, for practice. Kissing my knees felt funny, my shoulder like kisses Mom dispensed for goodnights and good luck before big tests. Kissing my own hand felt courtly. A duel knight, split at the waist, embracing awkwardly but at least new armor sparks in the clash. For now my desired boyfriend is more a dragon, unseen, untouched. I list the qualities I wish for, but I don't know what a boyfriend really is. How much is smoke, how much fire?

At the dormitory I wake up early to shower. In part I'm
embarrassed at how thin I am. My thin arms seem made to fit
inside the arms of other boys, an extra skeleton for them to use.
I wouldn't mind. Someone please put me inside. Mostly I don't
want to see the other guys naked. They intuit my glances and
turn more toward me, to mock me, the waterfall off their tan
stomachs rippling away into a forest of steam my eyes cannot
penetrate until I move in for a closer look. I won't allow myself
that move, a move toward a boy who moves away, smug in
the allure, powerful, now that he can name me, calling out to
the other boys just what I am. I can't even write that word in
my journal yet. I practiced it, the other day in algebra class,
over and over, in the reddest ink. Then I ripped up the paper
into tiny shreds. The only senior on our hall, Tony, the RAs
roommate, moves closer. I sense he has changed his schedule to
accommodate my averted gaze. His morning jogs come earlier
now, placing us more and more in alignment. He lingers, his
charged body casual against the shower wall, rivers of blond
hair fingering his brow under pressure of the white spray, always
facing me, legs apart; the water rushing between them molds to
the firm, handsome barrel of new flesh stationed there. He stands
there as if he were waiting, waiting for me, and that frightens me
more. When I shower in the morning I stand with my back to
him, directly beneath the showerhead as if it were an umbrella
shielding me from his storm.

Before the movie I head over to the one dusty record store in
town. I have been at school three months now and the owner of
the record store is the only person I've really talked to; he lets me
sit behind the counter and read his *New Music Express*. I don't
buy lunch some days so I'll have money to buy tapes. He's not
in today: it's the surly girl with too much mascara. I buy the new
Cure cassette and leave.

The movie theater has one of those old, broad marquees. The movie titles are in all capitals, like a declaration of something grand, more truth than title. The Baptist church down the street has a white peeling steeple and a sign smaller than the theater's, with moveable letters, too, wheeled out to face the infrequent traffic. SIN WILL FIND YOU OUT. Well, I am still waiting.

Choosing the horror movie, a sequel to one I haven't seen, I buy my ticket and push against the heavy glass door. Mercifully, the guy behind the counter doesn't ask for ID. Tired of getting carded for cigarettes, I buy them out of vending machines at the Denny's near campus. I've been old enough to see R-rated films for a year now but I look much younger than I am. Not just skinny, I'm short for my age as well. At theaters any boy my age or younger is cocked to card me; they do so with wide grins, looking down at me through the scratched glass of the ticket booth then back at my driver's license, always in some variation of ill-fitting shirt and clip-on bow tie; all movie theater employees are dressed like the harried members of a dispersed wedding party. Old men with baseball caps sit next to me during matinees. I'm eager for the previews so I rush past the conces-sion stand and into the first row. No one sits next to me if I take the first row, not enough cover. As the screen flickers to life I push my bangs out of my eyes. The previews are dull; no science fiction, one new horror film, it looks good enough that I'll look for it when it comes out. As the movie begins I recognize the mask of the killer; I *did* see the first film, loved it, in fact. The killer terrorized a hospital last time. Now he is resurrected by lightning at the mortuary and terrorizes a sorority across the street. He walks slowly and methodically down the hall as the girls run, full sprint. The killer somehow catches the hems of their pink nightgowns or ponytails and chops away. I think about my future boyfriend. I want him to be foreign, with an accent, and thick, curly hair. His fingers will taste like nicotine. He will approach me outside class to bum a cigarette. When he asks if I have a cigarette I'll say, "No, but I have a light." I can't make up my mind if that sounds ridiculous or seductive, or if the difference between the ridiculous and the seductive lies only in the response. Anyway, I like the idea of my boyfriend having curly hair, plus pouty lips. Next semester maybe I'll take French.

The movie ends before I realize it; only the blaring, bad heavy metal title song playing again alerts me that the film is over. The credits are rolling: *Girl #4, Girl #5, Girl Doing Laundry* and *Girl in Library*. Is this how the names of the girls they've fucked, want to fuck, said they've fucked, roll across the eyes of the boys in the dorm? I don't have or want any such numbers to put in columns, add or subtract, carve into statistics. I've wondered why they just don't make shirts, baseball jerseys to best display their prowess. I've listened to all their stories in silence; what I want doesn't seem as singular as anything that could reach a total, form in the ammonia stench of the faceless shower room. My boy will stand naked in my room in the middle of the night, taller than the darkness, leaning over me, kissing my open mouth. Hair falls onto my face and winds into my own hair, tightens, pulling him closer as his thumbs press into my chest, spreading my skin roughly, so hard it burns.

The theater lights go on. An usher walks to the front of the screen and stands, bored, hands-behind-his back, waiting for me to leave.

After ten o'clock curfew I smoke a clove cigarette in my room; we're not allowed to smoke but I begged my parents to pay extra so I could have a private room. I keep the window open and push towels up under the door so I won't get in trouble with the RA. Someone knocks on the door and I freeze. I'm glad the

tape I was playing has already stopped, the lights are out. I like
to smoke in the dark. Another knock. "Theo? Open up. It's me,
Tony." I'm silent, knees pulled to my chest, additional cushion
to my thumping heart. Then a whisper, "Theo, I smell smoke."
I get up and unlock the door and peer out. Tony is shuffling his
feet, wearing nothing but boxers, holding a towel. He's never
visited my room before. We have never spoken. I'm surprised he
knows my name. I open the door wider, saying, "Hey." Rushing
back to my bed I clutch the pillow and pull my knees back up to
my chest and watch him stand in the doorway, pause, look over
his shoulder then quickly enter. He locks the door behind him
and sits at my desk.

"No worries, Theo. I thought I smelled a clove cigarette and
was wondering if I could bum one." I point to the pack there on
the desk, he pulls one out and puts it in his mouth, it hangs there
like a comma; a silence grows as he relaxes into the chair, pushing
it back to face me. "Nice that you get to live alone. I mean, I like
my roommate and all, but since he's the RA someone's always
knocking at our door. No privacy, you know what I mean?" He
spreads his legs slightly—in the darkness I can discern the large
ripples across his boxers. I have seen this pair on him before:
loose and well worn, probably washed a thousand times, they
look as soft as clouds.

"Do you got a light?" He wags the cigarette between his lips.
I take the lighter from the nightstand and lean across the bed to
light his cigarette. In that quick illumination of instant flame I
look hard at his crotch, willfully searching out the mass coiled
behind threadbare cotton, his wide blond thighs open before me,
while with his deep inhalation fire catches the cigarette. As the
lighter flickers out I look up at his face to see that he is watching
me with approval. The room darkens and then grows lighter
as our eyes adjust. He exhales and relaxes into the chair. Legs

moved together, he seems to adjust his crotch, then leans back, legs now wide apart again. It is too dark for me to really discern his midriff and below. An idea catches in my throat. Swallowing nervously, I pause, trying to make my voice sound even, calm. "Do you want to hear the new Cure album?"

Tony exhales; his profile strong in a halo of smoke. "Sure." Fumbling with the case I insert the cassette into the small, battered stereo on my cluttered nightstand. As music sputters like a dying candle the tiny stereo light casts a blue glow about the room and there's a rustle of quick movement from the chair.

Tony is naked.

A velvet froth of black hair and his cock full and long, basking like a crocodile on the sandy beach of his thigh, turned just so, to expose the pulsing ridge of fine vein and taut foreskin. I can see everything, hand behind the pillow catching my crotch. "This sounds good," he says, and shifts, gold crocodile slowly withdrawing into the river of darkness between his open legs, to hover, a menace below the surface, before emerging again, sharp and hard, expanding, a sapphire tear of precum forming at the slit. Tony takes another drag. Behind my pillow I push my jeans down to my knees. My erection stabs the pillow. I finger the tip to taste the salt of my own tears. The music builds a dark bridge between us. I kick the jeans off from around my ankles and lay the pillow by my side. Tony exhales and shifts again, examining me in the blue light, T-shirt high up on my hairless chest; thin, bony waist; the brief ebony cut of pubic hair and my thin cock hard, white, held aloft by my thumb. He strokes himself. I stare hard, emboldened by my own exposure, rapt over his girth, the cuff of his foreskin. I want to move in but I don't. The next song begins as Tony stabs the cigarette out into the ashtray on the desk; the exploding cherry illuminates the spike of his nipple. His chest is broad, the striking indenture between his pectorals sacrosanct, perfectly curved and pointed as a temple's crest. Smoke hangs over him like a budding rain cloud. He straightens one leg and rests it on my bed, the sole of his large foot touching mine, towering over my small foot. His warmth is incredible, engulfing, electrifying. My whole body shakes. I can hear Tony's breathing grow shallow. He stops stroking himself and withdraws his foot; putting his hands on his knees he stands. Startled, I reach for my jeans but he calms me with a soothing hand on my ankle. He then squats by my bed, his open mouth close to mine. We kiss. Our teeth knock in a jarring moment quickly forgotten as he lightly bites my bottom lip, than places his open mouth over mine. Tongue grappling with tongue, the spice from his clove cigarette floods my mouth. His hand engulfing my cock I fumble for his, surprised at its strength and softness, fingering the silk of his foreskin, rubbing the salt of his precum across the head with my thumb. He groans; my eyes are open, his closed, his long, blond lashes sweeping my cheeks. I feel a tremor in his cock and wonder about my own impending explosion when he deftly leaps onto the bed, his weight crushing me; his body heat igniting me, I cum. My pelvis twitches under him, shooting ribbons now ground into my smooth stomach by his rigid one; lubing his hot cock in my sticky white molasses he increases his friction. So overwhelmed I can barely breathe, his Adam's apple grates my parted lips; I'm desperate for air.

Tony spreads his arms and rises as if he were doing a push-up only to pause, the quivering heat above my stomach mounting as his body tenses. I feel a surge from his shins resting atop my knees as his lightning strikes my chest. Tony exhales with a shudder and rolls off, collapsing on the bed beside me. I notice he is sweaty but clean while I am splattered with the resin of our encounter. The tape ends. Tony sits up. I think he is going to leave but he stands, reaches for his underwear from the floor, seems to consider something, lets the boxers drop and takes another cigarette from the desk. Cautiously, up on one elbow I flip the tape and pull my T-shirt off to mop up my chest and stomach. Tony settles down beside me, also on one elbow, cigarette hanging off his lips.

He is waiting for me to give him a light.

THE END OF THE GILDED AGE

Simon Sheppard

A miniaturist.

That's what you'd decided you were: a miniaturist. "I started out to be Basquiat," you'd said, "and ended up Vermeer." I smiled indulgently. I wasn't all that knowledgeable about Basquiat's work, and I figured that "Vermeer" probably overstated things. But you, working toward your MFA, had an ego that at least matched your talent. I, an undergrad in English Lit, was slogging my way through Edith Wharton.

"*Girl with a Pearl Earring,* right?" I'd cheated; I'd read the book. Ah, well, at least it was the book, not the movie.

"Yeah, though I prefer *Girl with a Red Hat.* So small, so perfect. And the light's amazing."

At that moment, I thought that *you* were perfect, the light in your eyes, your unfeigned enthusiasm.

We'd just had sex, were lying side by side on top of the rumpled sheets, the unmistakable smell of cum rising from our bodies. I'd always thought my "type" was some weedy, pale, dweeby boy with a sunken chest, but you were something quite else: Peruvian-swarthy, with a chunky, muscular body, smooth skin, and an uncut dick without an excess of foreskin. I'd seen you around campus, actually, and you later said you'd noticed me, but it wasn't till we locked eyes at the Gay/Straight Alliance dance that I realized how very much you turned me on.

We landed in bed just a couple of hours later, in your apartment in grad students' housing, you sucking my cock, then telling me that you were a miniaturist. Like Vermeer. Well, okay, I confess: anyone who gives me a blow job like that can be as pretentious as he wants.

You glanced over at my bedside table. "*God Hates Us All,*" you said. "You reading that for class?"

"Nah. For my own amusement, actually."

"You like it?"

"Yes, actually." I couldn't believe we were postorgasmically discussing literature. Well, yes, I could. This was college, after all.

"I hear Hank Moody's kind of a dick." You wiped some of your cum off your belly and licked your palm.

"Well, so was Picasso, or so I hear."

"I don't really like Picasso's stuff."

"Why?" I teased. "Too big?"

You reached over and gave my inner thigh a smack. Surprisingly, I liked it. Even more surprisingly, my dick started getting hard again.

You liked that. You took my cock, still damp with cum, into your beautiful mouth again.

I doubt that even Vermeer gave better head.

The next week, Jeremy killed himself.

Most of the campus had already gone home for the holidays, leaving a remnant of us stranded in a bleak Midwestern winter.

Truth is, I'd had a crush on Jeremy. He was, in fact, much more my type than you: tall, thin, impossibly cute. He had a boyish shock of dark hair that kept getting in his eyes, and lower down his whole torso was hairy, improbably so for a guy that young. Even his shoulders were a little hairy, and his ass, too, all his pelt dark except—I found out when we first had sex—the luxuriant pubes, unexpectedly on the blond side, that crowned his big cut dick. When I got him naked in his dorm room, I could barely believe I was so lucky.

He was, it turned out, rather passive in bed, at least with me; even submissive. He liked to suck my cock, sure, but he liked to be held down while he did it, his impressive hard-on bobbing against his lean, furry belly. And he also liked to be spanked, I learned; though I'd pretty much never done something like that before, with his encouragement, I happily turned his hairy ass bright pink.

I guess that's sort of kissing and telling, but I doubt he'd have minded. He seemed really at ease with who he was—more than I was, in fact. Afterward, he showed no embarrassment, no regret. He seemed utterly well adjusted, happy a lot of the time, which was particularly good for the rest of us because his smile was so, well, enchanting. Yes, absolutely enchanting. He was the furthest thing from a drama queen.

So when he took a header out of the fifth-floor window of his dorm room, it came as a shock. To me. To, apparently, everyone. There was no question he did himself in; he'd left a note, though apparently it didn't really say very much, certainly nothing that would Explain.

Jeremy was the first person I knew who'd actually committed suicide, but the things that were being said were familiar enough: "He had everything to live for." "He'd showed no hint that anything was wrong."

That kind of thing.

So yes, it might have been a cliché, but I couldn't believe it was true. Only it was true. Jeremy was dead. Forever.

People are, finally, mysteries. I didn't need a book to tell me that.

In the aftermath, I couldn't help thinking about his dorm room window, the same one I'd stared out of, after those few times Jeremy and I'd had sex. And I ghoulishly wondered if there'd been blood on the snow. I hoped there hadn't been blood on the snow.

Meanwhile you were gone, flown back to South America for Christmas with your family, who, you had told me, pleased themselves to believe you were engaged to a nice American girl.

After the first couple of postsuicide days, I found, somewhat to my chagrin, that I was becoming less and less upset over Jeremy, less distraught than I thought I should have been. Still, though I hadn't planned to visit my family, I grabbed a last-minute airfare bargain and went home for the remainder of the holidays.

The visit didn't go well.

I'd decided not to email you with news of the suicide—as far as I knew, you hadn't been close to Jeremy, anyway. So when you came back and I told you the news, you were not just surprised, but more upset than any of us, who'd already been living with the news for weeks.

I was surprised, too. Surprised to find out that you were in fact close to Jeremy, that you'd been in love with him. It wasn't all that improbable. It wasn't that big a school, after all, and there was a limited pool of gay guys to choose from, to fall into bed with. To fall in love with, comes to that. Hell, maybe I should have known. Or at least suspected.

"Don't cry," I said, but you couldn't stop.

I held you in my arms while you sobbed. Feeling you so close, so vulnerable, got me hard. Maybe I shouldn't admit that, but it's true. Hell, after a funeral, everyone goes and stuffs themselves full of food, so what the hell. The presence of death can sharpen our appetite for life, right? I'd read that in a bunch of books, and now I knew firsthand it was true. I wanted to strip you down then and there, to fuck your face, to slap your ass like I'd slapped Jeremy's. Still, I just held you, feeling your body radiate heat, keeping my erection discreetly out of it. After all, nobody wants to seem like an insensitive clod, right? Well, maybe I should say, "Few of us want to seem like insensitive clods." Just to be accurate.

You asked if you could spend the night with me, and I readily agreed. We slept spoons, and though we were both hard pretty much throughout, nothing happened. Not till the morning, when I woke up to find your mouth on my cock. There was a blizzard outside, howling through the campus, covering over the very last imagined traces of Jeremy's demise. I reached down for your big, responsive nipples, but you took your mouth away, said, "Just lie back," and then swallowed my dick all the way down to the root.

It felt so fucking good. After a few minutes, I said, "I'm really close," which was the truth, and you took your mouth off. I was throbbing, had to strain to hold myself back. Precum oozed from my slit.

Then you did something you'd never done before, something I wouldn't even have suspected you were into. "Turn over on your belly," you said, and when I had, you slapped my ass. Not hard, just enough for me to feel it. No one had done that to me before, at least not since the OBGYN did when I was born.

I'm not going to lie. I liked it. It didn't feel like I imagined it would when I did it to Jeremy. Oh, it felt like getting spanked, yes. Only better. Much. I guess I sighed. I'm sure I sighed. You slapped me a little harder, on the other cheek this time. It made for the damnedest combination of discomfort and pleasure I'd ever felt.

I let you continue.

You got between my legs, pulled my hard dick out from under me, and really got down to work. You went at the spanking methodically, ramping up the intensity, then pulling back, stroking my ass to encourage me to relax, then resuming, just a little bit harder. My sighs must have turned to groans.

I realized how amateurish I'd been when I'd spanked Jeremy. I also realized that you'd no doubt spanked Jeremy, too. For some damn reason, that thought made me want to come.

That and your spit-wet right hand on my dick, squeezing and stroking while your left hand kept up a steady rhythm of slapping my heated flesh.

"I'm really, really close," I said again.

"Just four more," you said, your voice not sounding like I'd ever heard it before.

You counted them out, slowly. Each of those four blows took an eternity. And the last two took me right to my limits.

But you were as good as your word. Once the ringing from the last slap had faded into the air, you easily coaxed me into shooting a load, squirt after vigorous squirt, onto my sheets.

After a minute, after you'd backed off and I'd caught my breath and the puddle of cum beneath my cock had started cooling, I rolled over.

You were crying. Crying again, though your cock was still hard. I didn't know whether to comfort you or blow you. So I did both. First I stroked your face. Then I reached over to your stiff brown shaft, and when you didn't flinch, I put my lips around the head and began to nurse on it. You relaxed, so I sucked you down. At one point, I felt what must have been a tear falling on my neck. It took you a while to shoot, long enough for me to lose track of everything in the world except your penis.

You didn't really respond, but you didn't call a halt, either. And finally, finally, you rewarded me with a mildly acrid load of cum.

Thank you, I thought. *Thank you so much.* My dick was still—maybe surprisingly—stiff but I didn't even care whether I came again or not.

You lay back on my bed. I stood up, the taste of you lingering on my tongue, and opened the curtains partway, then got back into bed with you and held you in my arms.

I was hoping you wouldn't start sobbing again. You didn't, but you were silent for a long, long time.

I stared at the window. The wind howled, swirls of snow in its grip. The light was a coldly watery white, like winter in Delft.

Finally, after I thought you'd drifted off to sleep, you spoke. In a furry, sad voice, your face turned away from mine, you said, "Jeremy. I feel so bad about Jeremy."

I stroked your face. "Shh," I said. "There's nothing any of us could have done."

"I should have known."

"Just because," I said, "someone likes to get spanked, that doesn't mean he's self-destructive." Which was the truth, but felt like self-justification, as well.

You turned to look at me. "He told me."

"What?"

"He told me he felt like killing himself," you said, "and I didn't do anything."

"You didn't think he would do it."

"Of course not. He was such a drama queen." The wind howled even louder.

Suddenly I wanted to come. I wanted it badly.

God hates us all.

COXED

Neil Plakcy

Jason Fitch made me hungry—deep down hunger, rising from the pit of my stomach, echoing in my throat, making my mouth water. He was that gorgeous: six-three, broad shoulders, shaggy brown hair and a goofy smile.

It was the first day of tryouts for the freshman crew team, a warm, sunny day in early September. The trees along the banks of the Schuylkill River were still green and cast changing patterns on the slow-moving river. Jason and I stood in a group of about a dozen guys at the boathouse, on the concrete apron that stretched out over the water, with a ramp at the far end.

All of the guys were big and strong like Jason, except me. I was a little runt compared to them. Though I am tough and wiry, I come from short people. I'm just above five-six, about a hundred twenty pounds soaking wet.

"Great, we've got a cox," the coach said, pointing to me.

One of the big guys giggled at the term, and the coach said, "For those of you who don't know, the coxswain is the key to a strong crew. He's in charge of steering the boat, motivating the rowers and coordinating their power and rhythm. You ever been a cox before, son?" he asked me.

I resisted saying that I had sucked a few cocks before, but never been one. Instead I just shook my head. "I'm too small to wrestle here, sir. But I'm strong and I have a big mouth, so somebody told me I should try out for crew."

He laughed. "Perfect attributes."

He showed us the shells. "Single sculls over there," he said. "In a race, there is either one, two, four or eight men in a boat. We also classify them by the position of the cox. They're either bow-coxed, stern-coxed, or straight."

A couple of the guys giggled over that, too. Yeah, any boat that had me in it sure wasn't going to be a straight one.

The coach droned on, and I could see most of the guys were itching to do something, and so was I. I kept looking at Jason, who was the real reason I was trying out for crew. He was in my history class, usually sitting in the row in front of me, and the couple of times we'd passed each other he had smiled and said hello.

Maybe that's not much to you, but a lot of big guys like Jason don't notice short guys like me. My head came up to his armpit, and it would have been easy for him to ignore me. But he'd flashed those pearly whites and said, "Hey," and I was hooked.

A couple of days before I'd heard him talking with one of his jock friends about tryouts for freshman crew. I thought I could get to know him better if we were teammates. Maybe I could even get into his pants. But if not, I'd get to sneak a peek at him in the locker room now and then, and that would be enough to fuel a few one-handed fantasies.

Finally, the coach sent us all into the locker room to change into our swimsuits. I tailed along behind Jason, taking a locker next to his. "Hey, you're in my history class, aren't you?" he asked, sticking out his hand. "I'm Jason."

"I'm Leo." I tried not to stare as he shucked his beige T-shirt, exposing a massive chest and flat abdomen. I pulled off my own shirt and hung it in the locker.

"You wrestled in high school?" Jason asked.

"Yeah. But the lowest weight class here is a hundred twenty five, and I don't want to push myself up that high." I looked over as he was shucking his shorts and boxers in one move, and his dick nearly took my breath away. It was long and fat, resting against his groin in a thatch of black pubic hair. "You rowed before?" I asked, trying to keep my voice normal.

"Yeah, in prep school," he said. "Coach was right. A good cox is the key to a strong team."

"I'll do my best," I said. I dropped my trousers, folded them, and placed them in the locker. Jason had already pulled his swim trunks on and was talking to a guy on the other side, so I took off my white Jockeys and hurried into my bathing suit, hoping no one would notice my budding hard-on.

When you wrestle, you get accustomed to touching other guys' bodies, and if you get hard, you just laugh. Our high school coach had given us a lecture once, all this crap about our bodies going through changes, and we shouldn't be embarrassed or worry if we popped a woody now and then. Some of the guys were proud of walking around the locker room naked and hard, like it made them some kind of big swinging dick.

Pretty early, though, I knew I wanted to do more with those stiff dicks than just tease their owners. But at the same time I knew that if I went too far while wrestling, I'd be outed faster than you can say cocksucker.

So I thought about math problems a lot when I was wres-tling, and that helped. Wrestling was all mechanical to me, and I could turn my brain away from my body and into anything else. I didn't think I could do that with crew, though. From what the coach said it was going to be a lot of thinking.

Without working at it too hard, I got myself assigned to a four-man scull with Jason. He was the biggest, so the coach put him at the far end of the boat from me. I sat facing the other guys, all three of them wearing T-shirts and bathing trunks, their legs stretched out toward me. The left ball of the guy closest to me fell out of his trunks as we were turning around, and it was all I could do to focus on calling out the cadence.

Jason's face was pure concentration as his arms moved smoothly back and forth. I wanted to reach out and touch the muscles I saw flexing in his arms and shoulders. I wanted those arms wrapped around me.

The other four-man scull tipped over at the turn and dunked all the guys in the water. We laughed, but focused on finishing our race. We were almost back to the dock when the first guy facing me realized his nut was getting an open-air tour, and when he dropped his oar to adjust himself, we took a wicked turn and I went flying. Fortunately it was close to the end of practice, and I was able to get into the shower and wash the river gunk out of my hair.

"So, you like it?" Jason said. He was at the shower next to mine. I looked over at him and saw his dick, once again half-hard and hanging down. For a minute I thought he was coming on to me, right there in the showers, but then he said, "Crew, I mean. You like it?"

"Yeah," I said, almost gasping for breath. "I think it's gonna be cool."

We practiced a couple of times a week during the first month of school, and I often found myself hanging out with Jason, either on the walk down to the river, or in the locker room. In history class, he moved back a row so that he was sitting next to me, and sometimes I got so distracted looking at the way his dick seemed to pulse against his pants leg that I missed whole lectures.

One Friday afternoon we were leaving practice and Jason said, "You going to the party at Phi Theta tonight?"

I shrugged. "Don't know."

"A lot of the guys are going," he said. "It's a big crew frat. You should come. It'll be fun."

"Okay," I said.

"Want to walk over together? I'll meet you under the arch at eight."

I agreed, and the rest of the afternoon I was very excited. Sure, it wasn't exactly a date with Jason Fitch, but he definitely gave me a vibe. Maybe he just wanted to be my friend—but friendship can come with benefits.

The party was loud, with music blasting and people yelling, and smelled like sweat and spilled beer. Jason and I hung out together, talking to a couple of girls, and a few other guys from the crew team. I downed my first cup fast and went back for a second, starting to feel a nice buzz. Jason was pounding the beers too, and it must have been after my fourth one that I suddenly had to pee badly.

"Know where the bathroom is?" I yelled to Jason.

"Gotta be one upstairs," he said. "I gotta drain the lizard too. I'll go with you."

We muscled our way through the crowd to the staircase and hurried up it, both of us desperate to empty our bladders. We passed a couple of bedrooms, then saw the door to the bathroom half-open. "You go first," I said. "I can hold it."

"Ah, come on, we can both go at the same time," Jason said. He rushed into the bathroom, opened his fly and started to pee.

Seeing him, I couldn't hold back. I barely got my fly open and my dick out before the urine was streaming out of it. "Damn, that feels good," Jason said, arching his back. "Feel good for you, too?"

He was looking down at my dick. It wasn't as big as his, but it was thick. As he looked, his own dick stiffened. He shook the last drops from it, and then touched his index finger to his lip and wet it. Then he stroked the finger down the length of his dick.

I looked behind him. The door to the bathroom was still half-open. I shook my own dick, then without putting it away I stepped behind Jason and closed and locked the bathroom door. Then I put my hand on his stomach.

"Dude," he groaned. He grabbed my hand and moved it down to his dick. Very gently, I ran my finger around his piss slit, teasing it. He pulled me close to him, nestling my head against his chest, and leaning down to kiss the top of it. I grabbed his dick with my hand and started jerking him as he shuddered and whimpered.

He came fast, spurting his cream into my hand. I looked up at him and smiled. "You liked that?"

"Oh, yeah," he said. He picked me up then, as if I was nothing more than a heavy book bag, and stood me on the lip of the tub. I still wasn't quite at his height, but it was easier for him to lean down and kiss me on the lips. And as he did, he reached for my dick, which was painfully hard by then, sticking straight out of my pants and rubbing against the harsh zipper.

He pulled my dick all the way out of my briefs and pants and started jerking me. I was having trouble breathing, panting and kissing him, and my whole body shook with the power of my ejaculation.

"Pretty awesome, huh, dude?" he whispered into my neck, as I spurted into his hand.

"Fucking A," I said.

And then, it was just like we were in the locker room, cleaning up after a practice. We used somebody's scummy washcloth and went back downstairs for another round of beers.

It must have been one o'clock when Jason stumbled into me. "Think I might have had a little too much," he said. "Having trouble keeping my balance."

"Lean on me," I said. "I'll get you back to your dorm."

He gave me this crazy smile and said, "Lead on."

We started singing on the walk back to his room, "Staying Alive" by the Bee Gees. I don't know if he started it or I did, but we were both having a blast. As we got to the dorm, though, I put my finger to my lips to quiet him. He grabbed the finger and put it up to his own lips—then sucked on it.

"Oh, man," I said. "You have a roommate?"

"He went home for the weekend."

Jason took off running, up the steps and into the dorm, me right behind him. Nobody was out in his hallway, and he fumbled with the key, then popped the door open and stumbled inside. I followed him, and as he fell onto his bed I dropped right beside him.

We were both fully clothed, but I could feel how hard he was through all those layers. He scrambled on top of me, kissing me, grinding his dick against my leg. I knew a couple of wrestling moves, though, and quickly I had him pinned under me, our beery mouths locked together. We rolled and struggled, laughing, and ended with me sitting on top of him, feeling his stiff prick against my ass.

Jason reached up, untucked the tails of my good party shirt, plaid seersucker, and then reached his hands up under the fabric to my stomach. I loved the feel of his hands against my skin. I unbuttoned the shirt and then shrugged it off, as he reached up to tweak my nipples.

I arched my back and groaned as the tension snapped from my little brown nubs directly down to my dick. Jason was wearing a chocolate-brown polo shirt, and I pulled it off over his head and then leaned down to suck his nipples. I could feel his heart pounding in his chest, hear his ragged breathing in my ear.

"You have a rubber?" I asked breathlessly. "I want you in me."

I rolled off him and pulled down my pants and boxers, as he reached over to the table next to the bed and pulled out a rubber and some lube. I unbuttoned his pants, unzipped him, and then nestled my face down against the fabric of his jockey shorts. I licked his dick through the fabric and then shimmied his pants and jockeys down.

His dick was magnificent, hard as steel, pointing back up toward his stomach at a 45-degree angle. But I didn't need to think about math; all I wanted was that dick inside me.

I moved back over him, sitting back on his legs, facing him. I took the condom from him and grabbed one end of the package in my teeth, ripping it open. I pulled the limp wrapper out, then opened it and positioned it over the head of his dick.

With a quick motion, I slid the whole thing down over him and he yelped. Then I squirted some lube on his dick and started rubbing. "Dude," he said. "That feels so good."

"It's only going to get better," I said. I leaned back and took his right hand in mine, then squirted some lube onto his index finger. "Loosen me up," I said, leaning back and showing him my asshole. "Get me hot and juicy for that big dick of yours."

His fingertip danced around the outside of my hole, the nail just gently grazing my skin. "Come on," I said. "Stick it in me."

"Two can play your games, you know," he said. "I want you to beg for it."

"Dude," I said. "I'm begging you. Please. Stick that finger up my ass."

He laughed and obliged, wiggling it around so that the walls of my channel were coated with the lube. Then he squirted some more lube in his hand, as I balanced above him, and he stuck a second finger up there.

He's a big boy, Jason. Big everywhere. Big dick, big feet, big hands. That second finger really stretched me, and I felt like I could sense every inch of his skin, and his fingernail scraping so gently up, up, farther into me.

I couldn't wait any longer. I pushed his hand aside and lowered my ass down onto his dick, wincing and taking deep breaths. He was so big, bigger than any guy I'd taken up there before. But all that loosening helped, and after a half-dozen tries I got him all the way inside me.

"Oh, man, dude," he said. "That is so awesome. God, don't stop doing that."

I went up and down on his dick, clenching and releasing my ass muscles. He cried out and whimpered as I pistoned up and down on his dick, then he grabbed my dick and started jerking it. I was so hard by then that the touch of his hand on me sent me into spasms, quickening my breath as waves of heat flashed through my body.

Jason squeezed his eyes shut and howled as he let loose a load into the condom's reservoir. I could feel his dick pulsing against my insides, the extra pressure of that come inside the latex. I came just after that, spurting into his hand and on his chest. The orgasm was so intense I almost blacked out, the heat welling up inside me.

I slid gently off Jason's dick and rolled over next to him. "That was awesome," he said. "I never...you know...did that before."

"Any of it?"

"The ass part," he said. "Damn, that was better than any blow job."

"Glad you liked it," I said, rubbing my hand against his chest. I snuggled my head against his skin, and he wrapped an arm around me. Within a couple of minutes he was dead to the world, mouth open, snoring like a band saw.

I squirmed out of his embrace, pulled my clothes on, and snuck out of his room.

I didn't see him again until Monday morning in history class. I was freaking out; I worried that he'd move to another chair, that he'd snub me. I'd have to drop crew. What if he made up a story for the rest of the team?

But he walked in like nothing had happened. "Hey, Leo," he said, sliding into the chair next to me. "How's it going, dude?"

"Pretty good," I said. "How about you?"

He opened his notebook. "Got majorly wasted Friday night," he said. "Must have passed out as soon as I got back to my dorm."

So that was how we were going to play it, I thought. I could deal with that.

We had a test scheduled for Friday, and Jason asked if I wanted to get together and review. "They've got these private study rooms in the library," he said. "A buddy of mine was telling me about them. You just sign in at the desk, and you can shut the door, lock it even, until your time's up."

Okay, was that some kind of coded invitation? I wondered. "Sure," I said. "I need to get up to speed on Alexander the Great anyway."

Our class was History 101, from Alexander's rise as king of Macedon until the fall of the Roman Empire. Our professor had already told us that the first exam would focus on Alexander's early years, his conquest of the Persian Empire, through his death.

I saw Jason again at crew practice twice, as well as in class on Wednesday, and he didn't say anything beyond confirming our plan to study, meeting at eight in the library. He'd already reserved the room, he said.

Thursday night I met Jason outside the study room, which had an automatic lock that had been opened for him by the clerk at the desk. "Isn't this cool?" he asked, showing me the door. "We can lock ourselves in, and nobody can bother us until our time is up."

There was a long, narrow window in the door, but you could pull a shade down on the inside for privacy if you wanted. I followed Jason in the door, both of us carrying our heavy textbook as well as our notebooks and laptop computers. He pulled the privacy shade down and locked it in place.

The room was smaller than a dorm room, with a round table in the center and four chairs, as well as a shelf nailed to one wall. We stacked our crap on the table and sat down. I powered up my laptop and found a refresher quiz on Alexander on line, and Jason and I took turns testing each other.

"What was the name of the eunuch from the court of Darius III with whom Alexander had an intimate relationship?" I asked Jason, after we'd been studying for close to an hour.

"Bagoas," he said. "That's grim, isn't it? Being a eunuch? Gives me the shivers."

"Me, too," I said.

"Can a eunuch—you know—do it?" he asked. "I mean, they cut the nuts, right?"

I turned to Google. "Yeah," I said, after a minute. "Supposedly you can still get a hard-on. You just shoot blanks."

"You think Alexander was gay?" Jason asked, leaning back

in his chair and stretching his long legs out.

I shrugged. "Gay is like, really a modern thing," I said. "I think back then, men had sex with men and they didn't put a label on it. I mean, Alexander was married twice, right?"

"Three times," Jason said. "Roxana, Stateira and Parysatis. He even had kids, didn't he?"

"Yeah. But they say his longest relationship was with Hephaestion," I said.

"Must have been wild," Jason said. "Soldiers getting it on."

"Mmm," I said. "Those hard bodies. Like yours."

I could see his stiff dick pressing against his jeans. To make sure I noticed, he put his hand on the fabric and dragged it even tighter. I reached over and put my hand over his dick, feeling it hot and throbbing beneath me. Jason groaned. "We ought to study," he said.

"I'm studying this," I said. I leaned down and nuzzled his groin with my nose, inhaling his funk. I unzipped his pants and pulled his dick out.

"Oh, man, you make me crazy," he said.

I teased the tip of his dick with my tongue, snaking it into his piss slit, then slobbering up and down his shaft. "Dude, you make me so horny," he said, as I licked and sucked him. He pushed my head down on his dick and I swallowed him to the root, then started bobbing up and down on him.

His whole body began to shake and he was panting like a dog left in a hot car. He shot off in my mouth with a suppressed moan, and I swallowed the whole load.

I sat back in my chair, smiling. "We've still got more studying to do," I said. "We need to bone up on the spread of his empire."

"Bone up," Jason said, smirking.

"We may have to reserve this study room again tomorrow

night," I said. "I mean, even after the test, we might need to do more boning."

He reached over and stroked my hard dick through my pants. "For a little dude, you've got a big boner," he said.

"You want it?"

He smiled. "Yeah, I do." He leaned down and rubbed his head against my groin, like a big shaggy dog. I unbuttoned my pants and pulled my dick out, and he rubbed his chin against me. His stubble chafed against my sensitive skin and I yelped.

"It's the library," he said, looking up at me. "Shh."

Then he started to suck me, and it was all I could do to keep from moaning and whimpering. I'd never been with a guy who was willing to give as well as he got; most of my sexual experience had involved giving blow jobs and hand jobs, then jerking myself off afterward. I liked sex before Jason—but I loved it with him.

He wrapped his lips around my dick and pulled in his breath, creating a vacuum, and pulled up like that. Then he repeated the process. I'd never felt such sensations on my dick, and I exploded quickly.

Jason swallowed everything I had to give, then sat back with a silly grin on his face.

I looked at my watch. "We've got this room for another hour," I said. "We could do at least two more practice quizzes and still have some time left before we have to check out."

Jason smiled slyly. "I like the way you think," he said. "And the way you suck cock, too."

"Baby," I said, "this is just the beginning."

MY SEVEN-INCH TOY

Donald Ammer

It had been my best birthday gift in some time, courtesy of a sister who didn't know any better—a portable DVD player with a seven-inch screen and remote, plus a battery that was good for running at least two and a half hours before recharging. Not the best brand—or the highest-end product—but perfect for what I'd been dying to use it for, for about three months now: porn. Growing up in a small northwest Indiana town, even being gay, you still didn't have much access to smut—not as long as you had parents who monitored your Internet activity, anyway. Thank god for my friend Charlie, whom I'd met the previous year when we were both freshmen at Ball State; that dude was into porn the way the Colonel was into chicken. He'd given me a bunch of his old male-male porn DVDs last year, when we'd parted company at the end of the semester, and from then on we'd become close friends (even if he did live in Oklahoma the rest of the year).

But being at home with my parents and two younger sisters—

and a busted DVD player in my bedroom, thanks to a sister who'd dropped it—made for no privacy during summer break. Even my PS2 wouldn't play anything X-rated.

So when July and my birthday came around, the *numero uno* gift on my wish list was a portable DVD player—something I could watch my porn on, in bed, with my headphones plugged in, in the privacy of my own space. And—go figure—my bratty teenaged sister Christy came through.

In the two weeks before heading back to college, I watched all-man sex on that poor little DVD player every single night— pulling out my own six-and-a-half-inch prick to beat my meat to the action I watched on the seven-inch screen. I nutted some- times two, three times a night to porn, and had even gotten to where I was experimenting on myself with some of the things I'd seen on DVD—fingering my own ass until I came, eating my own jizz...and, thanks to a very willing cantaloupe out of our kitchen refrigerator, even cutting a hole in a melon and fucking it.

To this day, I sometimes wonder if my sex education, in those two weeks, had topped what I'd learned in "regular" college the entire previous semester. I didn't even feel the desire to date, or have a boyfriend—neither of which I'd ever done before. Not as long as I had my portable DVD player with the seven-inch screen, and the stack of forgotten porn that Charlie had almost thrown away.

Wow, was I naïve.

I was almost dreading going back to Ball State for sophomore year, because I knew this semester I would have an apartment in town that I would be sharing with three roommates—which meant sharing a bedroom with at least one of them. Assuming most or all three of the guys were straight—or even if they weren't—this was bound to put some restrictions on my nightly bedtime cinema. *Oh, well,* I thought, trying to be philosophical, *my dick could use the break, anyway.* Summer had sucked, and I was determined to make the new school year the best I could.

I moved into the two-bedroom apartment the weekend before classes started and met two of my roommates right away. Andrew was a biology major, a tall and kind of geeky redhead with prominent front teeth and about a zillion freckles. The other guy at the apartment when I got there, Edward, was a really hot jock with thick brown hair and a Clark Kent kind of look about him. I don't remember, to this day, what he was studying—but I do remember that, when I met him, he'd just gotten out of the shower, and all he was wearing was a white terry-cloth towel around his waist—which he had no problem removing as he went into his bedroom to get dressed, revealing a totally nude and very athletic frame...and, quite possibly, the prettiest dick I'd ever seen. Shit, was Edward going to be a distraction.

And of course, Andrew and Edward had already copped the first (and biggest) bedroom for themselves—leaving me the smaller room. It was clean, with a pair of twin beds and small computer desks to match—and not much else. I had my laptop, clothes, all my stuff moved in within the hour—taking the bed farthest from the bedroom door, of course—and basically spent the rest of the day getting to know my roommates...and wondering where this "Keiran" guy, the fourth roomie (and my bunkmate), was.

It had been a long day driving downstate, so I gave up about eleven, told the new roommates goodnight, and went to bed. My DVD player had been charging all day, so I knew the battery was good, and there was a Jet Set Men movie I had that I hadn't watched in some time—so I crawled into bed a happy camper, alone and ready to enjoy myself. Wearing only a white T-shirt,

I propped the DVD player on my chest and adjusted the towel I was lying on (so that I wouldn't stain the sheets when I nutted), then stretched my long legs wide—bent at the knees, in case I felt like a little ass-play, as well.

The scene I wanted to watch featured two blond muscle dudes who fuck a dark-haired, barely-legal college kid in a locker room. My boner blossomed soon as the scene started—as it always does—standing straight up from my thin but well-toned body (I work out at least three times a week, no matter what), and I was just getting down to business...when I heard the doorknob turn on my bedroom door.

I freaked, slamming the screen down on my little DVD player and shutting it off at the same time. Scrabbling for the blankets, I managed to cover myself up just in time—rolling onto my side to keep my dick from standing up like a tent pole under the covers—for the bedroom door to open and the light to flick on, a harsh yellow glare that made me squint and raise one hand to shield my eyes.

Keiran had arrived.

"Oh, man, I am so sorry if I woke you up," he said, struggling into the room with two huge duffel bags and a laptop case slung over one shoulder. "I'm just going to drop my stuff and go right to bed anyway, man—I'm exhausted."

And he did just that—setting the laptop on the spare desk and shoving his heavy duffel bags over into a corner of the room on his side. Then he came over to where I still lay in bed, squinting up at him.

"Hi," he said, bending down to extend a hand. "I'm Keiran."

"Ben," I replied, shaking his hand with the very same hand I'd just had wrapped around my dick seconds earlier. "Nice to meet you."

My eyes had adjusted by now—and boy, was I blown away by my new roommate. He was either Indian or Pakistani—olive skinned, with a head of thick, wavy black hair and huge, very expressive dark brown eyes. Amazingly good looking, Keiran had a large nose and big, kissable lips that worked to create a sensually masculine, almost too handsome face. That, combined with his lean swimmer's build (he must have been six-two or taller) made Keiran total model material. Even his voice was deep and warm—kind of husky, sensual.

I'd never seen anyone like him before—not in my white-bread hometown, not in my previous year at school...not even in my beloved porn. And wow, was I turned on.

"Like I said—I'm heading right to bed," Keiran told me. "I'm bushed." He went over to his bed and tossed back the covers... as I adjusted my own blankets up to my chin, to make sure my portable DVD player was hidden beneath them. As I watched, Keiran flipped off the light switch again and went back to his bed, kicking off the sandals he wore (his feet were at least a size 12, I noticed, long and dark and clean, with tiny black hairs barely visible on his toes). Before getting into bed he stripped off the gray T-shirt and jeans he wore, down now to wearing nothing but white briefs that—even in the shadowy bedroom—stood out brightly against his dark skin...and showed the outline of a very well-developed dick, even soft. I watched in fascination, unaware that I was even staring, as Keiran got into bed and rolled over to face away from me. Shit, even his ass was perfect—round and big, but not too big. His body was, as I'd guessed, smooth and well-toned—a swimmer's physique. My erection, which had softened a bit, had now grown back to full size again, aching for action. So much so, I was truly disappointed—seconds later— when Keiran pulled the covers up over his perfect body and that hot ass, evidently planning to go right to sleep.

I sighed, rolling over onto my back again in bed. I was hornier than ever, so ready to stroke and shoot my load—maybe even taste it again—but suddenly, for the first time, jacking off just didn't seem like enough. And I really didn't wanna risk getting caught by the new, probably straight roommate the first night out anyway.

So, grudgingly, I placed my DVD player on the floor next to my bed, shoving it a bit underneath so I wouldn't step on it by accident the next morning. My lube was still in the bedside table drawer next to me, but I made sure to grab the Jet Set Men DVD box from the bedside tabletop, hiding it under the bed, as well—

Oh, shit. I realized now that the DVD box had been lying out, in plain sight, on the bedside table when Keiran had come over to shake hands with me. He *had* to have seen it—and god knows, the two muscular guys kissing on the front cover left little to the imagination as to what kind of film it was. And yet—he'd said nothing, made no indication that he'd seen the DVD box at all.

I lay there thinking, mind blown by the whole thing, when Keiran suddenly spoke in the darkness. He still lay in his bed, covered up, his back to me—but I heard him loud and clear.

"I don't normally sleep on my side," he said matter-of-factly, "so when you're finished jacking off, could you let me know?"

My jaw dropped open. All I could do was stare at Keiran's back, not even ten feet way from me in his bed, as he suddenly rolled over to face me—those big, dark eyes boring into mine.

"Unless, of course," he said, "you'd like some help instead?"

He stripped off his briefs and crawled into bed on top of me, cock already growing hard as it pressed against my own rigid erection. Rolling my T-shirt up and off my body, Keiran then bent his head and sucked my lower lip into his own soft, thick-lipped mouth, his tongue entering my mouth at the same time, probing. It was the sweetest kiss I'd ever known, heartfelt and sensual, and I found myself wrapping my own lips around his, pulling back wetly on his mouth as my own tongue danced with his, tasting him. When his lips moved down my chin—across my throat—lips and teeth and tongue tasting every inch of flesh it found, I wrapped my legs around his waist, ankles crossed and my size-10 feet holding his ass tightly to me, pressing his crotch into mine.

His mouth moved southward, soon tickling at my belly button, and seconds later he'd wrapped those thick lips of his around the head of my cock, tongue flicking as he swallowed farther down, taking me all the way into his throat. I gasped, bucking my hips into his face; no one had ever sucked my dick before, and the sensation set off a fire in my gut.

"I wanna suck your dick," I whispered, voice shaky. "I—I wanna suck your dick, man. Please."

My legs released him as Keiran maneuvered around to lie next to me, upside down now so that his big, brown uncut cock hovered right in my face. He was huge—maybe nine inches or more of rock-hard dick that curved slightly to the left, pointing back down at my bed. Side by side it was a tight squeeze, the two of us in a twin bed, but as soon as he inhaled my boner down his throat again, I tentatively took his oversized prick in my hand as well...pressing my body into his as I slowly took him into my mouth to complete the sixty-nine.

He was musky but not dirty, tasting of pure manhood and a little hint of sweat thrown in like spice. He tasted and smelled of sex, and I worked hard to get him all the way down my throat, careful not to use my teeth. I was already fucking his mouth, gagging him, and as soon as Keiran knew I was used to his giant prick down my throat, he began thrusting with his hips into my face, too. I tried not to choke on him but he was just too big—so after a few minutes I rolled over on top of him, where I could control how much of his cock I took into my mouth...as, by now, I was also hammering his throat—already close to orgasm just from fucking that dark, handsome face of his.

"I want you to fuck me," Keiran suddenly said, my cock popping from his mouth. He was gasping for air, tonguing my balls and going for my asshole even as he spoke—his big hands already spreading my pale ass wide. "I want your dick inside me. Please," he repeated, voice husky....

And then I felt his tongue enter my ass, and it was like the fourth of July was going off in my head—all bottle rockets and white flashes and multicolored lights exploding in my brain. Never had I felt like this—like liquid silver flowed through my very veins—and I let Keiran's big dick fall from my mouth as I moaned out load, feeling his tongue bury itself deeper into my hole until my heart was racing so fast, I thought it would bust out of my chest.

"Oh, my god," I moaned, settling myself farther onto his face and riding my hole up and down his wet tongue. "Oh, god, that feels so goooooood...yeah, tongue that hole...deeper...oh, yeah, eat my assssss...."

And suddenly, all I wanted to do was fuck him.

He had condoms and lube in his duffel bag. As I lay his long, dark and well-built body out on my bed, on his back—his thick legs spread as I knelt between them, rolling a rubber onto my dick and lubing it up—I felt a stab of fear go through my guts, and thought it best to be honest.

"I'm a virgin," I told him. "I—I've never fucked a guy before. Or been fucked. So kind of bear with me, okay?"

He smiled. God, was he hot. "Just go slow," he said. "I

haven't gotten fucked in a long time, myself—so go slow, and we're cool. You're sure you wanna do this, Ben?"

My pale eyes met his dark sensual ones, and I nodded. "Yeah. I'd definitely love to fuck you, man."

I knew it was important that he be relaxed, so as I shuffled closer to Keiran on my knees, I took both his ankles in my hands, putting his big feet together. Then, as he watched me, I lowered his large feet toward my mouth, and sucked both his big toes in between my lips at once, sucking hard and licking in between them. Keiran hissed, even tried to pull his feet away—but I held firm, mouth tightening around his big toes, tongue sliding in between them and then over to his right foot—my mouth tasting and licking in between each of the digits on his size-12 foot. Eventually he relaxed, letting me have my way with his feet, and I found myself totally getting into him; shit, even his *feet* just tasted incredible. As I worked them over, licking the soles of both feet up and down and tasting those toes until they were shiny with my spit, I noticed that Keiran's huge dick had grown even harder. It was now bouncing off his flat belly as if on springs, a fat, dark uncut sausage that left a trail of milky precum on his stomach with every bounce.

I wanted to watch Keiran as I entered him—wanted to see there, in those big brown eyes of his, what it felt like to have my cock invade his ass. So when I felt he was relaxed enough, I draped his feet over my shoulders and generously lubed up two of my fingers...before slowly pushing them inside his big brown ass.

"Oh, shiiiiiiiiit..." Keiran moaned, chewing on his lower lip. I watched my pale fingers slide into that tight, dark hole and felt my erection bump up another notch. Man, was he tight—his asshole clenching like a vise around my slim fingers as I gently forced them in to the second knuckle. Keiran sighed, spreading his legs wider to accommodate them, his hands clasping his legs under the knees to hold them higher, pulling them into his chest so I could get my fingers in even deeper.

I fucked him for a few minutes with my fingers, ramming them harder with each thrust, building up speed until he was gasping on my bed—head thrashing back and forth on the pillow, the handsome, hunky East Indian guy still chewing on his lower lip in pleasure. Finally, I couldn't stand it anymore, and slowly slid my fingers out of his butt...pressing my lubed-up, condom-covered cock at the very edge of his hole, instead. Bracing one hand on either side of him on the bed, I lay on top of Keiran and allowed his legs to slide high up over my shoulders...then slowly guided my cock into that hot, tight little asshole of his, barely forcing the fat head in.

Keiran gasped, pushing at my shoulders with his big hands, trying to shove me away. His eyes, wet with tears, met mine— Keiran still chewing on his lower lip—but he said nothing so I pressed in harder, forcing more of my cock deep inside him, then fell down on top of him before he could push me away again, kissing the guy whose ass I suddenly wanted to *possess*.

His arms slid around my shoulders and then I was fully inside him, fucking him, Keiran gasping for breath in my ear as my lips left his to nuzzle at his neck. His moaning in my ear only turned me on more, and—like the countless men I'd seen in porn after porn film—I withdrew my cock nearly all the way before plunging in again, building up speed and really getting into that tight ass of his. Keiran grabbed my face and we were kissing again now, mouths devouring each other, all the while my cock hammering faster and faster up that hot hole of his, Keiran gasping and wheezing and whimpering between kisses, his arms tight around me as I plunged harder and harder up his ass, my orgasm building....

And then my back arched and my head flew up and I crammed all I had up that ass one last time—feeling Keiran's legs tighten over my shoulders—and then I was coming, my cock erupting like a firehose up and into the condom I'd crammed up Keiran's ass, jet after jet of white-hot cream blasting from my piss slit and into him as my body went rigid, and my eyes saw black, and I just kept unloading up his stretched, violated hole.

I fell onto him again as I felt the last of the jizz drain from my balls, knocking the air from Keiran's body as we shared a few sleepy kisses. Our bodies were sweaty and sticking together, the room smelling of man-sweat and sex—and I wouldn't have had it any other way.

We rested about ten minutes, cuddling in my bed, before Keiran announced his desire to take my ass cherry. I must have said no about twenty times before finally giving in (the truth was, I really *did* want him to fuck me with that big dick of his)—and over the next hour Keiran initiated me into the fine art of being a bottom. It was the best sex ever—even better than my topping Keiran—having that big, dark cock plunging repeatedly up my white virgin ass as I watched…and when Keiran finally nutted, all over my chest and stomach, I rubbed his cum into my skin like lotion.

We showered together afterward, careful not to wake up Edward or Andrew, and I gave Keiran a blow job in the shower that caused him to blow yet another huge load of cream in my face. When we'd dried off, Keiran invited me into his bed—mine was too trashed and stained—where we fell asleep nude, with me lying on my side and facing my bed, Keiran spooning behind me with his arm around my waist. Never had I felt warmer in my life; warmer, or more at peace.

The last thing I remembered seeing before drifting off to sleep was the corner of my little silver DVD player with the seven-inch

screen—still sticking out from under my bed on the other side of
the room. My intro to male-male sex on film...and my gateway
to male-male sex in real life.

I hoped, now, that I could retire it for a while.

THE STACKS

William Holden

His name was Vincent, an undergraduate at the university and the newest pledge for the Alpha Gamma Gamma Fraternity. He was here in Special Collections researching the history of the fraternity. I'd seen him a few times around campus with his brothers-to-be, and had always been amazed that the sorority girls were not falling all over him with his dazzling good looks and gym-toned body—that is until the students started talking. As a librarian you hear things from the students; I guess they figure you're safe and not a threat. Word around campus was that Vincent was a player, quick hookups with nonsorority girls was his thing. He wasn't one to get tied down with the same girl, and none of them ever got more than a first date. His brothers-to-be bragged about his sexual conquests, yet the girls all say that he never fucked any of them. It had become a bit of a contest to see who could get him first.

I was sitting behind the reference desk trying to concentrate on my own work when suddenly I felt that I was being watched. I looked up and caught Vincent looking my way. He quickly looked around the room at the other researchers before returning to his work. His black dredlocks were shorter than most and appeared a bit loose. They hung over his forehead and with his head down he seemed to use them as a cover for his wandering eyes. His light brown skin, the tone of a mocha latte, appeared soft and flawless. His dark green T-shirt fit tightly over his body. I let my eyes drift down below the table. His brown shorts stopped just above the knees. His legs were covered in a blanket of dark hair that trailed off just above his ankles.

It was a few minutes before closing time, and the other researchers were packing up for the day, Vincent didn't seem to notice. I stood up, walked over to his table and squatted down next to him.

"We're getting ready to close," I whispered to him. "Would you like me to put these materials on hold for you?" He appeared surprised at my closeness.

"Thanks, that would be great."

I pushed the cart containing the materials he was using back into the stacks area. As I returned to the desk he began to pack up his laptop. He walked by me and smiled but said nothing else. I watched him as he signed out and headed down the hall to the elevators. The door opened. He glanced back in my direction before stepping in. I sat there for a moment letting my lonely mind play with the possibilities as the last of the researchers walked out.

I sat in silence for a moment, glad to have that part of my day over, but knowing that I had a long night ahead of me. I was working on an exhibit on the lives of the queer beat poets. I have always had a strange curiosity for the lives of Allen Ginsberg, Peter Orlovsky, Neal Cassady and Jack Kerouac. So when I was asked to curate an exhibit of their lives, I couldn't have been more excited. I didn't realize at the time however, how many late nights I would have in the library putting the pieces of their lives together.

I began gathering the materials I had been pulling from the various collections then stopped and decided that a workout in the campus gym was what I needed before settling in with the poets for the night. I locked up the twelfth floor and waited patiently for one of the elevators. As I rode down to the main level of the library I began to think about poets. I had always had a secret crush on Kerouac and kept a postcard of a photo taken in 1957 that showed him with Peter Orlovsky, shirtless on a beach in Tangiers. I could vividly see in my mind Kerouac's strong chest with a small patch of hair nestled between his pecs. His wet trunks stuck to his body, revealing the heft and size of his cock. The elevator door slid open and brought me off of the beach. I walked through the library and out onto campus hoping no one would notice the bulge that had started to form in my jeans. I adjusted myself as discreetly as possible.

The campus was alive with students as they went about their semester schedules. I always tried to workout during times when the students were less likely to be there. It wasn't that I didn't like seeing these young college men all hot and sweaty after a workout, it was just the contrary. I liked it a bit too much, and I worried that my over-anxious libido would get me into trouble. So I played it safe. I only worked out in the early morning before most students were awake, or right after work when students were either in class or having dinner.

The gym as usual was relatively empty as I walked in. The smell of young sweat, mixed with that of chlorine, filled the air. I walked back to the locker room to change. There were a few students in various stages of undress hanging around with their friends. I tried not to stare as I made my way to my locker. I noticed several eyes glancing my way as I walked past them. It was nice to think that at the age of forty and with my salt-and-pepper hair, I could still get a few looks from the young men. My cock stirred restlessly with the thought. I quickly changed and headed into the workout room for a round on the elliptical machine. By the time I had finished the workout, my shirt was soaked with sweat. The locker room and showers were empty as I made my way to one of the stalls.

As I stood in the shower letting the hot water cascade down my body, I felt once more as if I was being watched. I stuck my head outside the shower curtain—no one was in sight. I grabbed the bar of soap and began lathering my skin when I felt that uneasy feeling of being watched again. I suddenly noticed that I had not closed the curtain completely. I looked out of the small opening and I noticed someone in the shower across from mine. His curtain was also open at one end. Most of his face and body was hidden behind the curtain. The black dreds behind the curtain were a dead giveaway—it was Vincent.

My first thought was to close the curtain, but the thrill of leaving it open overcame my initial thought. I knew I could never hook up with a student. I couldn't risk losing my job for a few hours of hot sex even if it was with one of the sexiest students on campus.

I watched him from the four-inch opening in my curtain, hoping to get a glimpse of his body. I stood there nearly paralyzed with growing desire. Without thinking, I let my hands move down my chest and stomach, massaging the soap into the hair that lay damp against my skin. I reached farther downward, rubbing the water and soap through the mass of tight curly pubic hair. My cock responded to my touch and his darkened silhouette, beginning to thicken in my grasp. I continued to look through the small opening and saw the movement of

Vincent's arm pressing against the plastic curtain. The thought of him stroking his own cock, running soap through his pubic hair, sent a warm rush of pleasure through my body. I watched him out of the corner of my eye as I rinsed the soap from my body. Suddenly, as if he could read my most secret of thoughts, he raised his hand and grabbed on to the shower rod. My eyes made contact with the thick, black hair that gathered under his arm. It was long and swirled against his skin. I licked my lips and wondered what it would taste like to run my tongue through the soft, silky hair of his freshly washed armpit. I couldn't take it any longer. I knew I was getting close to crossing the line that shouldn't be crossed. I closed the curtain, turned off the water and began to dry myself off.

I wrapped the towel around my waist and reached for the curtain to open it. I paused wondering if Vincent would be there. I could almost feel his presence, his energy, standing on the other side. My mind returned to the darkness of his armpit. I could almost smell the freshness of his youthful body. My cock began to press against the towel before I could force the thought away. I took a deep breath and opened the curtain. The shower he had stood in only minutes before was empty. I stepped out of the stall and looked around. He was nowhere to be seen. I walked back to my locker, hoping no one would see the stiffness beneath my towel.

By the time I made it back to the library, the evening had turned dark. The library was deserted except for a few dedicated students still studying. I stepped into the elevator and unlocked it so it would take me to the secured floors. As it began its slow, mechanical climb my mind drifted back to Vincent in the shower and the raw energy that poured off of him. I took a deep breath to refocus on the job at hand. I stepped out of the elevator and into the closed, dimly lit stacks. The silence was a welcome relief as I walked the length of shelving to the area where the materials for the exhibit were being temporarily stored. I picked up one of the personal diaries of Neal Cassady and began leafing through it, reading about his secret desire for and love of Kerouac. I began to imagine the two of them together alone in a room. I pictured Kerouac standing in front of Cassady in nothing but a flimsy pair of white briefs. They both looked at me as if I was standing in the room with them. I could feel Kerouac's eyes on my body, secretly undressing me. He appeared nervous, as if unsure about his desire to be with another man. I looked past him, farther into the room, and saw Vincent standing there with us. He was wearing the same brown shorts and green shirt I remembered him wearing earlier that day. I shook my head trying to get Vincent out of my fantasy then realized he wasn't merely in my mind. He was here with me. His darkened silhouette stood at the end of the row staring at me. He moved toward me. His footsteps echoed softly against the tile floor. He moved closer. I could hear his breathing beating against the silence of the room. The scent of his freshly showered body drifted through the stacks, teasing my loneliness. My desire for him returned. He came up to me and stopped. The silence was deafening. I wanted to reach out and touch him, to feel his skin next to mine. I rubbed my fingers together in nervous anticipation. I needed to break the silence before it sent me over the edge.

"How did you get up here?" My voice was more accusatory than planned.

"I saw you come back up here after the gym." His voice crackled with nerves. "I told the security guard that you were expecting me tonight to help you with your project, so he let me up."

"Why?"

"I think it's pretty obvious," he said as he closed the space between us.

I could feel his warm, sweet breath beating against my face. The heat of his body surrounded me. I watched with surprise and nervous excitement as he grabbed the edge of his T-shirt. He pulled it up and over his head. My heart leapt into my throat. He tossed the shirt to the floor. His body was smooth except for a few tufts of hair surrounding each nipple and a narrow treasure trail that drifted down from his navel and into his shorts. I resisted the temptation to touch him.

"But..."

"No buts. No questions." He leaned over and placed his lips upon mine.

Everything melted: my resistance, my worries and my heart. I gave in fully and completely to my desires. I opened my mouth and let his tongue slip inside. It was warm and thick as it caressed my tongue. His hand grabbed the back of my neck. He pulled me further into him. My heart pounded in my ears. I was sure he could hear it, like a jackhammer running at full speed.

I pushed us apart to catch my breath. The air was hot and stagnant. The scent of our overheated bodies hung heavily around us. His eyes were piercing. I could feel them drilling into me. He grabbed my shirt and ripped it open. The urgency and suddenness of his movement caught me by surprise. The sound of my buttons hitting the tile floor echoed around us. He ran his hands over my chest. His fingers moved through the tangles of sweat-dampened hair that covered my body.

I grabbed him and pushed him down onto a pile of cardboard boxes. He lay there looking up at me, his hands intertwined behind his head. A smile crossed his face. I could smell his deodorant working overtime. Its metallic sweaty scent drifted up to me. It pulled me in, to a place I knew I should not be going. I removed the torn shirt from my body. I kicked off my shoes and unbuttoned my jeans.

I watched as his eyes explored my body. His eyebrows arched. His eyes got larger as he noticed the bulge of my crotch stretching the thin white material of my briefs. I stepped out of my jeans and lowered myself toward him. Our bodies were separated by less than an inch. I leaned down and kissed him. I licked his thin, soft lips; kissed his neck, his shoulder. His scent became stronger. I looked at him. The tip of my tongue slipped out between my lips. I moved to his armpit. His scent overpowered me. My tongue moved through the mass of black hair already damp with sweat. The muskiness of his body invaded my mouth. I inhaled deeply, bringing him into me. I became dizzy with his smell and taste. I pushed farther into his armpit, licking every inch of him. I nibbled at the tender flesh below the hair. His body shook. A moan escaped his throat as I moved to his other side.

He grabbed my head and pulled me off his armpit as his body shook again. We looked into each other's eyes. He paused as if wanting to say something but pulled me down to his lips instead. I opened my mouth. He greedily licked his own sweat and muskiness from me. He broke our kiss. He looked at me—into me. His lips formed as if he wanted to say something again, but no words formed.

I moved down his body. His nipples, large and erect, became my temporary toys. I nibbled and sucked on them. His body rocked and arched with mine. I moved farther down, tasting the salty flavor of his stomach. His hands gripped my head guiding me downward. My mouth found the beginning of his treasure trail. I followed it with my tongue, knowing where it would lead me.

I reached the waistband of his shorts. I could feel the pulse of his cock beating behind the material. My right hand ran up his leg. I looked up his near-naked body. He was watching my every move. My hand slipped under the material of his shorts. I caressed his inner thigh. His body trembled. A moan drifted down to me. My hand went farther up his pant leg. The heat of his body intensified within the confines of his shorts. His underwear was damp. My hand made contact with his long, thin cock. My heart raced and my cock swelled with desire. Sweat beaded up on my forehead and chest. I pulled myself off of him and unlaced his shorts, pulling them, along with his underwear, off in one forceful tug.

I stood up and looked down on him; his naked body shiny with sweat and aroused by my touch lay before me. His thin, uncut cock lay erect against his stomach in a puddle of precome. I pulled my underwear off and let the heft and weight of my cock hang freely.

His hand reached up and wrapped around my cock. His grip was firm. He stroked me. My cock grew in his grasp. He gathered my precome on his fingers and slipped them into his mouth. I watched him lick my moisture from his fingers.

I spread his legs and lay down between them. His youthful manly scent drifted around me. I licked his fuzzy balls. His body shook. I slipped one nut, then the other into my mouth. I rolled them around, feeling the skin and hair against my tongue. I reached up and grabbed his cock. I stroked him. Pinching the foreskin together I pulled and tugged on the layers of skin.

"Fuck, that feels good," he panted. "You've got one hot mouth."

I released one ball, than the other. They hung heavily from his body. Wet with my spit, they glistened in the dim light of the room. I looked up at him and smiled as I raised his hips and ran my tongue to the hairy, tender skin just below his sack. I pushed his hips farther up and saw his tight pink hole surrounded by shorter curly black hair. The tender puckered hole trembled in anticipation. I licked it. The muscles contracted. I licked it again, longer, deeper than the first. His muscles relaxed. I watched as the muscles opened and closed. I lowered myself again. My tongue slipped in. His body convulsed. My tongue went deeper, enjoying the feel of the soft, silky flesh of his ass.

He grabbed my head and pushed me farther in. "Damn, that feels good. Yeah, that's it. Tongue-fuck me. Yeah, come on. Eat my ass!" he growled. The hot moisture of his ass covered my tongue.

I could feel the muscles in his ass loosen, allowing me full access. I pulled up, my face wet with spit and sweat. I crawled up his body. Our cocks met for the first time. I let him lick my face and lips before kissing me.

He reached down behind me and pulled his legs into the air. I looked at him and could tell that he wanted me to be his first. I kept my eyes locked on his. I pulled myself up and grabbed my cock at the base. It was hot to the touch and the veins pulsed with an urge I'd never known before. I moved the head of my cock over his wet hole and applied a little pressure. He grimaced slightly then relaxed.

He nodded. I slipped farther inside of him. We rocked together back and forth until all nine inches of my cock were deep inside of him. I could see the pleasure in his eyes, hear the desire rising in his breath as I began to fuck him.

I could hear the creaking and tearing of the cardboard boxes beneath us, but my desire for Vincent outweighed my concern for the materials. I noticed the picture of Jack Kerouac on the beach, lying next to Vincent. His eyes seemed to follow our movement. He was watching us fuck.

I grabbed Vincent's cock and began to stroke him. Precome

poured out of his long, slender cock, wetting my hand and the mass of tight curly pubic hair. Our bodies were soaked with sweat. Beads rolled off my face and fell onto Vincent's chest. I bent my head lower and slipped the head of his cock in my mouth as my cock went deeper inside of him.

The muscles in his ass began to tighten. His hips moved in frantic waves as I ran my tongue around the tip of his cock.

"Holy shit!" he groaned. "I...never...felt... Oh, fuck!"

I could feel his cock swelling. I knew he was getting close. I let his cock fall from my mouth and righted myself to fuck him full-on. He grabbed his cock and started jerking it. The sight of our bodies took me to the edge.

"Yeah, that's it, Vincent, jerk that cock. Yeah, fuck your ass feels good." I panted and moaned as my orgasm reached its limit. "I'm going to shoot!"

"Yeah, give me your hot load. Yeah, come on, fuck me!"

My body tensed, then trembled uncontrollably as the first round of my orgasm unleashed into him. I could feel him tightening his ass muscles, milking my shaft for more. I fucked him harder, my cock getting firmer as another full load shot into him. I looked down and saw my come pouring out of his ass covering my cock and pubic hair.

"Shit!" was all Vincent could say before he exploded a long thick stream of come across his chest. I continued to fuck him, enjoying the second and third blast of come from his cock. I fell on top of him. Our overheated bodies came together in a puddle of sweat and come.

We lay there in silence, our breathing heavy and labored. To my surprise he turned his head to me and kissed me. There was no urgency, no heat of the moment. It was gentle, soft and passionate.

"I want to see you again," he said as we dressed.

"But what about all the girls I hear about?"

"They mean nothing to me. I only date them because I'm trying to get into the fraternity. No matter what the guys are saying, I never have and never will fuck any of them."

"I'd like to see you again as well," I replied as I wrapped my arms around his body. "We just have to be careful. We can't keep doing this in the library."

"We won't," he said with a wicked little smile. "Next time we'll do it in the frat house." He winked at me as he walked away leaving me alone in the stacks.

COLLEGE DIVE BAR, 1:00 A.M.

Natty Soltesz

Hey, man—how's it hangin'? Yeah, you can sit next to me.

That paper for communications class? No, I didn't do it yet. My girlfriend'll probably do it for me. Yeah, she's smart as hell, helps me out all the time. Long as I'm givin' it to her! You know what I'm talking about.

No, she's out of town, visiting her parents. So, yeah—no pussy for a couple days. What're you gonna do.

Look at this place. I came here to pick up chicks, but it's a fucking sausage fest. There was this chick earlier I was talking to—she's actually in our class. Big tits, kinda obnoxious voice, sits in the back with that other chick…yeah, that's the one. Whatever. She was looking pretty tore down. Yeah, I woulda hit it anyway, but oh, well. Probably for the best.

Anyway.

Hey Lyddie, can I get two more shots please? Southern Comfort. Thanks.

Yeah, it's no big deal. I'll probably head home after this and pork my roommate.

You know him, right? Dean? Dude, don't look so shocked. Yeah, I fuck him. It's a pretty sweet deal I got going on, actually. Just slide my cock right up his ass and go to town. He's tight as hell.

Shit, man. Quit looking at me like that. Maybe I shouldn't have told you. It's really no big thing.

Hell no, I'm not gay. Is he gay? I don't know…maybe. But he's got a girlfriend and everything so…

Yeah, dude, he loves it. In fact I know he's fucking waiting for me right now. He'll probably have his ass in the air by the time I get home, all fuckin' lubed up and ready to roll. I just ram it up in him and go to town. He digs it, man, fuckin' cums all over the place before I even finish. Lets me jizz right inside him too. Not like he can get pregnant or anything, right?

How long has it been going on? Geez, I dunno—maybe a couple years? Since we were roomies in the dorms down the hall from you, I guess.

It just sorta happened one night when we were drunk. We were at the bar—in fact I'm pretty sure it was here. Yeah, cause Lyddie used to get us in even though we were underage.

We were talking and it was pretty late and we weren't getting any play. You know, typical freshmen with absolutely no game.

Dean started talking about how we should just go back to our room and jack off. He had a new porno or something.

"I'm fuckin' tired of jacking off," I said, and Dean was like, "We can slip on some rubbers and fuck the mattress." Honest to god. I was laughing but he was totally serious.

"It's better than using your hand 'cause you can hump the shit out of it. Just stick a bunch of hand cream in the rubber and stuff your cock between two mattresses." I was dying by this point. Dean's a fucking whack job; he's always coming up with crazy shit.

So I'm like, "Sure, let's do it, I don't got anything else going on." We go back to our room—we stopped at the 7-11 on the way and got some rubbers and KY—and we're all hard and horned up. Dean's got the tube of KY and he's squeezing it onto his cock like it's toothpaste. Then he does the same for me and he starts rubbing it in and I'm like, "Dude, just keep doing that and we'll be fine." But he's like, "Fuck no; I'm not jacking you off." Which—well...whatever. It just isn't his thing.

So we lube up our cocks and slide on a couple of rubbers and stack our mattresses on top of each other. We're fucking naked and hard and we kneel down side by side on the floor and stick our dicks between these mattresses. And I'm laughing but at the same time it's actually kinda hot. The rubber keeps your cock from getting all scratched up, and it's full of lube so it's wet and squishy and the weight of the mattress is pretty tight.

I look over and Dean is going to town; he's got his knees kind of spread apart and his butt is sticking out. I'm getting into it too and Dean looks over at me and just smiles. We start showing off for each other, like taking it slow, pinching our nipples as we sweet-fuck our mattresses, taking our cocks almost all the way out and slamming them back in. Dean's watching me and I'm watching Dean, and you know he's got this kind of beefy butt...it really looks good as he's backing it up and rocking it forward. I guess that's when I started to get the idea.

Now I knew that Dean liked to have stuff up his ass when he came. Sometimes when we were jacking off his fingers would sort of roam underneath his balls, and just a week or so before all this happened I caught him when I came home; he was beating off with a Sharpie marker stuck up his butt. He was kind of embarrassed but I didn't care. I've tried it. Who hasn't tried it?

So anyway I started thinking what it might feel like to have my dick up Dean's ass. And at that moment, sliding my cock in between a couple of fucking mattresses, for god's sake, it wasn't hard to imagine that it would feel pretty goddamn good.

So I started testing the waters. I scooted closer to him on my knees, and he scooted closer to me, so our hips and thighs were sliding against each other as we humped. It gave me a better view of his cock anyway and him of mine—actually he was staring pretty hard core at my cock. Which I can't really blame him for. I've got a big dick. No bullshit. It's a honker.

I started saying shit. "Work that bitch, man. Fucking get that cunt." It sounds stupid but it was turning both of us on.

My hand was right there so I just reached over and put it on the small of his back, you know, to sort of help his hips along, to egg him on. He did the same for me and eventually my hand like naturally slid down to his buttcheeks. He didn't freak out or anything so I kept it there, and after a while I started dragging my fingers along his asscrack. Dean's totally smooth, totally hairless. Fuck, I'm getting hard just thinking about it.

Yeah, Lyddie, I'll have another beer. Yuengling, please. And a shot. Two shots. Sweet.

So I'm all-out touching his ass but Dean's still fixated on my cock. So I take his hand and bring it out in front so he's cupping my balls. He sticks out his fingers so he can feel my shaft sliding in and out from between the mattresses. And that's when I knew that this could possibly go the way I wanted it to, but still I'm not sure.

I'm like, "Dean, I can't believe we're doing this shit. Fucking a mattress, it's pathetic." And Dean's like, "I know." We both laugh and the mood breaks. I get up on the bed and lie back, and Dean lies down beside me and we peel off the condoms.

"Here we are," I say, "two fucking hard-bodied jocks and no warm hole to stick our dicks in. Isn't there anything we can do?"

I know, I was being totally obvious but Dean wasn't willing to make the connection.

"That's not entirely true," he says, and I look over at him, stroking my dick to keep it hard. "We've both got warm holes," he says.

And I'm like, "Yep, that's true." For a minute we just lie there stroking our dicks which are so, so hard. We both knew what was coming but neither of us could get up the nerve to say it.

"I wonder what it would be like," I say. And Dean's like, "To what?" "To have a dick up your ass," I say. I'm like, "I've never had anything that big up my butt before. Have you?" And Dean's like, "Yeah, basically I have."

"Does it hurt?" I say.

"Maybe at first but once you get used to it it's fine." Another minute goes by where we don't say anything and then Dean's like, "Actually it can be pretty great."

Now I'm thinking, "Okay, this is definitely going to end with my dick up Dean's ass. But I gotta get there without making him feel like he's, you know, fagging out or whatever."

So I say, "Dean, you know we're best friends. Whatever happens in this room stays in this room. If what you're saying is true, then that could end up being a pretty sweet arrangement for the both of us." Still he's quiet, so I take a different approach.

"I don't know, though," I say. "I don't know if I could stick my dick up a guy's ass. Seems pretty dirty. Even Trisha"—that's my ex-girlfriend—"even Trisha used to want it up the butt but I was weird about it because it seemed gross."

"It's not gross," Dean says. "If you wash it and everything and keep it clean. I keep mine clean."

"And you like, shave yours and everything too, right?"

Dean's like, "Yeah." So I'm like, "Lemme see." Dean rolls

over onto his stomach. "Raise your ass up a little bit," I say, and he does, so his cheeks are kinda spread open. I take his ass in my hands and I spread his cheeks apart even more and there's his hole. It's fucking pink and tight looking and I'm fucking throbbing hard, just thinking of getting inside it.

I say, "Yeah, it looks pretty clean." Dean says, "I just took a shower before we went out so it should be." I can't smell it or anything; it just smells like Dolce & Gabbana, which is Dean's cologne. And suddenly I've got this overwhelming urge to eat him out. Hey, what can I say? I was thinking of it like a pussy. I wanted to stick my dick in it, so why not stick my tongue in it, too?

So I get a little closer and sniff around. It really doesn't smell bad, maybe a little musky, but not bad. I tell him that. Then I touch it with my tongue just to get a sense. Dean bucks forward, just goes nuts at that little bit of contact. "Tastes okay, too," I say. "You mind if I try some more?"

"No, man," Dean says, so I did. Worked my tongue right into his butthole, and it wasn't bad at all. Different taste from pussy but pretty much the same.

Don't knock it if you haven't tried it, man.

So Dean was fucking loving it, just whimpering and whining and scooting his butt back onto my tongue. I mean, I had him, man. No doubt.

I came off and Dean's wiggling his ass back at me like he was trying to get in anything that would fit. I ran my finger across his asshole, just teasing him with the tip, and he rocked back so that my whole finger slid inside. Then I said, "You're gonna let me fuck you, aren't you?" He didn't say anything so I slapped his ass a couple times as I pumped him with my finger. "You want me to bonk you, right?" He's like, "Uh-huh." And I'm like, "Finally."

Shit, last call. You want another shot?

Four more, Lyddie, please. Yeah, Southern Comfort. What? Two are for him. We're walking home, don't worry.

Anyway, so I grab the tube of KY, get myself lubed up as hell and him too, and stick my fat hog right at the entrance to his ass. I take my time because I'm pretty sure he's like, a virgin—at least to male-to-male fucking, which I was, too.

I'm taking it slow and finally the head of my dick gets gobbled up by his ass. He's like, "Take it out, take it out," so I do and he starts trying to back out completely. You know, "I don't know if I can go through with this, man," and shit, to which I'm like, "No way." I mean, we've come this far. My balls are starting to go blue. Come hell or high water I'm going to get it in there.

I start teasing him with the head of my dick and he digs that. Pretty soon I manage to work it back inside. This time it comes easier for him, so I slide more and more in. Then, soon enough, I'm balls-deep inside him.

How can I even describe it? Sweet. As. Hell. The fact that this is my *buddy*, you know? Not some chick I had to get drunk or talk to for hours before taking her back to my room. This is my fucking lacrosse-playing, bitch-railing stud of a roommate, and I'm going to fuck him as hard as I dare, because I know he can dish it out just as bad as I can.

I mean once he got past that initial pain I pretty much had free rein. I was long-dicking him, sliding out and pushing all the way back inside. I reached down and he was completely hard, still. I put him on his side and fucked him like that, his cheeks hugging the sides of my shaft as I fucked his butthole. He rode me for a little while. We stood up and did it against the wall. That might not have been all that night. Actually I think we came pretty quick that first time, but we've done it so much since then I get it all confused.

I mean, yeah. We do it a lot. When we don't get chicks, anyway. Actually sometimes we just do it anyway, 'cause it's easier than finding chicks. It's like the fast food of sex. Some mornings I don't even have to roll out of bed. I just call him over and pork him till we both cream.

Fuck, they turned the lights on. Guess it's time to split. Where you headed?

Oh, I didn't realize you had a place off-campus. That's pretty sweet. You live by yourself? That sounds all right.

Motherfucker! I just remembered! Dean split this afternoon; he went home to his parents' house for the weekend! Fuck, guess I really am hard up then!

Well, you got any beer back at your place? Fuck yeah, man— I'll drink anything. Drink anything and fuck anything. You know how it is.

So you got half a case of beer and the whole place to yourself. Got any mattresses we can fuck? Ha, ha. But seriously. All this talk. I need to get off.

Hell man, you play your cards right and you never know who will bend over for you. Yeah, even me. No biggie, man—I let Dean have a crack at it from time to time. Be pretty selfish if I didn't. How big are you? Lemme check…shit, dude. That's some dick you're hefting around in those jeans. Oh, well. We can take our time, right? Got all night. I'll teach you how to eat some ass, get me ready. I'm saying, you play your cards right and you can pork me all night long. Good thing we ran into each other, huh? Otherwise we'd have been at home beating off alone instead of you have a nice, juicy ass to plug.

Don't sweat it man. How's this—I let you take me out to breakfast tomorrow morning. That's a pretty good deal, right? Beats an expensive dinner, and lets us get right to the good part. I'm a cheap date, all right? I'm not ashamed to admit it.

KISS-IN

Rachel Kramer Bussel

I used to envy my parents' generation, those who'd gone to school in the sixties, when everything was peace, love, understanding, orgies and social activism, when students were inspired by more than where their next paycheck was coming from. It's not that I wanted there to be another Vietnam, but I wanted to be part of something bigger than myself. When I finally got to college, I discovered that, unlike back in high school, there was plenty of that energy to go around, and on the first day, I joined the gay rights group, thankful to see that it was populated by all sorts of guys, many of them extremely hot. Well, extremely hot if you're me and into big, hunky bears. It's not that I don't appreciate a well-muscled chest and six-pack, but give me a man who can pin me down and rub his fur all over me, whose beard tickles my skin when he bites my nipples, whose body heat could keep me warm in an Alaskan winter, and I'm his.

I quickly started seeing Zeke, the leader of the group. He, of course, had guys practically lining up to blow him, but for some reason he took a shine to me. Not that I'm hideous or anything—I'm five-eleven, with sandy blond hair and freckles, an average body—not bad, but nothing special.

We decided to stage a kiss-in in support of gay marriage, and asked all students, straight, gay, bi, whatever, to join us. It didn't have to just be guys locking lips with guys (though seeing that en masse would be enough to give me a major hard-on); the point was that kissing, love, sexual expression and marriage are things we're all entitled to. Plus, frankly, it sounded fun. We scheduled it for right after the last midterm, when everyone would surely be needing a break, wanting to let off some steam and show the administration that we were a force to be reckoned with. Plus, those who were coupled up could indulge in a little PDA while those who weren't might have the chance to hook up, kind of like being under the mistletoe at Christmas, except our whole student plaza would be covered in a kind of political mistletoe.

Zeke and I agreed to pose for the poster, and got our art student friend Brendan to photograph us. At first, we were wearing T-shirts and jeans, but Brendan convinced us to ditch the shirts. Feeling Zeke's sweaty, hairy chest made me growl, and Brendan's camera clicked faster. I briefly opened my eyes and saw a video camera trained on us; apparently, Brendan had an assistant, but by that point Zeke was twisting my nipples in such a delicious way that I wasn't really paying attention. "Keep going," Brendan encouraged us, and when Zeke's hand reached for my cock, I didn't stop him.

"Show it to me, Dean," he said, his gruff, deep voice making him seem much older than twenty. Our two-year age difference often felt like more to me, and I sometimes imagined Zeke was older, and so did he. He liked me to call him Daddy when I begged him to fuck me, and had even lashed his favorite leather belt across my ass and "punished" me for infractions like a bad grade or forgetting to take out the garbage. So I was used to following his orders, just not in front of other people.

When I slid down my zipper and my erection popped out— I'd stopped wearing my boxers when Dean told me he preferred guys who go commando—he whistled. "I bet if these politicians had a chance to get up close and personal with that they wouldn't be so quick to want to limit marriage to a man and a woman." I thought I heard a soft "yeah," echo across the room, but I wasn't sure. "Close your eyes, Dean," Zeke told me. I did, instantly, then felt him pushing my jeans down my legs. I heard footsteps coming closer, and knew my hard cock was on display for everyone. Zeke's hand reached for mine and wrapped it around my shaft. I was under his spell, but also, I admit, the spell of the cameras. I'd never really thought about it before, but the idea of hundreds of my fellow students seeing my dick like this, seeing how hard Zeke made me, seeing two real, gay guys getting it on, had a certain arousing charm all its own.

I heard whispers and slowly brought my hand up and down, using my other hand to play with my balls. Soon I felt a suspiciously smooth pair of lips kissing my balls, a hot tongue traveling up my shaft, and a much smaller hand than Zeke's palming my package and stroking me. The fact that the person giving me a blow job wasn't Zeke was confirmed moments later when Zeke kissed me, his pierced tongue shoving its way into my mouth. His lips covered mine for a moment, making it a challenge to breathe, but I didn't mind. We'd never really talked about seeing other people, only commented on which guys in our grade were the hottest, but it felt good to simply look and not touch, and as long as I had Zeke's blessing, I wasn't going to turn down a blow job, especially an on-camera one. Zeke

slapped my chest, the sting of his fingers on my nipples rever-
berating through my body.

He bit my lips, bit my tongue; pinched the skin of my upper
arms, my chest, my stomach while someone, either Brendan
or his assistant, deep-throated me. I couldn't take it for much
longer than a few minutes, and as Zeke pinched my nipples
extrahard, I came, pretty sure no mouth could swallow that
much come. I was right, because when Zeke said I could open
my eyes, I saw the assistant looking up at me with thick milky
liquid dripping down his chin. I reached down and pushed some
of it into his mouth. He shut his eyes and let me, then sucked
my fingers deep into his throat. I didn't even know his name,
and no one volunteered it, so I didn't ask.

They left and Zeke and I took a shower, during which he
spread my cheeks and sank his cock deep inside me, his balls
slapping wetly and loudly against my ass. I loved that we were
so in sync, that we didn't need to overanalyze every detail of our
sex or our relationship. We could chill in the library for a few
hours studying, occasionally passing notes, go to dinner in the
cafeteria or go to parties or readings or rallies, but also have the
hottest sex imaginable. None of my high school boyfriends—all
two of them—could hold a candle to him.

And then the photos showed up. I'd thought we'd be in
profile, that we'd be two anonymous guys swapping spit, but
somehow, flyers posted in every conceivable spot on campus
showed me with my eyes shut, Zeke's mouth at my nipple;
another one had us mid–deep tongue kiss, and another showed
him pulling me close. They were hot and intimate and they were
the new advertisement for our protest.

Pretty soon the X-rated version was making its way through
campus, too. Thankfully, because the videographer had been
too busy blowing me, I wasn't the newest gay porn star on

campus, but it seemed that everyone from professors to super-straight cheerleader types to the guys I'd lusted after from afar had seen me getting it on. Well, anything for a cause, right? The campus paper asked to interview me and Zeke, and we invited the reporter to Zeke's place.

"Do you really think getting so explicit is going to help the cause of gay marriage?"

Zeke looked at me, smiled, then said, "Well, we think kissing is a part of marriage, and we also think that most students on this campus are already pro-equality. What we want is for them to come out in force, en masse, at the protest to prove it, to put their bodies where their politics are. We want to show the world that unlike the public image of us as middle-of-the-road students more interested in partying than anything substantive, we have something to say. It's not just a gay issue; this affects everyone, and all you have to do to get involved is pucker up. In public. If we did it, so can you." And then he got up, walked over to my chair, and gave me a loud, lusty kiss, with plenty of tongue, one that lasted for about a minute.

I sucked in a deep breath when he was done and looked timidly up at the student reporter, Jake. "I think I've got everything I need," he said, and scurried out the door before I even had a chance to see if we'd given him the hint of a hard-on.

Well, I soon found out that he was so quick to leave because he planned to make us a cause célèbre on campus, turning us into poster children for gay rights. Two days later, I awoke in Zeke's arms to a ringing telephone, and eighteen emails asking about the soon-to-be-infamous article. It showed one of the most erotic of the PG-rated photos, and went into detail about our kiss and our relationship, making us seem like gay-sex rock stars, taking activism to a new level on our campus. Soon the local papers were calling, even the nightly news. The press didn't

let up for the whole week leading up to the protest, and many of
those calling were less interested in the details of our event than
the details of what Zeke and I got up to behind closed doors.

On one hand, it was an invasion of privacy. I wasn't used
to being the poster boy for anything. On the other, being able
to hold up an example of gay love, even if we weren't ready
to get married ourselves or anything like that, made me truly
proud. We were kissing for a cause—and turning on reporters,
students and professors alike, judging from the comments we
got. One professor who I'd suspected might swing my way
asked me to stay after class, then stammered his way through
a compliment on our dedication before trying to put the moves
on me. I panicked, glancing around, sure someone had seen.
I knew he could get in trouble for even so much as touching
the back of the neck the way he had, let alone pulling my hips
close enough to his to feel the solid erection he was packing,
but I might be subject to disciplinary action too. I couldn't
afford that.

The night before the kiss-in, Zeke and I did much more than
kiss. I was determined to show him that even though, now more
than ever, there were guys blowing up his cell phone, bombarding
him with email, staring longingly after him (and they weren't
all out or even queer, necessarily, he was just that hot), I was
the one he should be with, I was the one he should pick. Alone,
we weren't trying to please or placate or politicize anything. We
just wanted to fuck, and suck, and spank, and indulge. Or at
least, that's what I wanted. Zeke apparently wanted to show me
his new leather belt. The one he'd bought with me in mind. The
one he told me would go perfectly well around my wrists, or
ankles, or being slapped across my ass. "Which one should we
start with?" he asked, a deceptively light, yet slightly malicious,
tone overtaking his voice.

"My wrists," I said, because much as I longed to be spanked, I love being tied up. I love seeing what he's going to do and not being able to stop it. I love giving him the power he craves, showing him that he is everything I want and need. This was no longer a casual relationship for me, as evidenced by the jealousy that raced through my body when I saw the other guys who tried to get a piece of Zeke. He shoved a pair of his dirty briefs in my mouth, then slapped my cheek lightly before moving behind me to secure my wrists. I was already naked; he'd made me strip upon walking in the door. Having his underwear in my mouth meant, sadly, that I couldn't suck his cock, but I liked the muffled sound of my screams as he fastened clothespins to my nipples. Apparently Zeke did too, because he laughed, then took out his giant cock, waving it in front of me as if to say, "Ha ha, you can't have this." I pleaded with my eyes, but that was all I could do.

Zeke took out some lube and started jerking himself off, slowly, as if we had all the time in the world. My dick spoke for me, standing straight up, showing him how turned on all this made me. Just when it looked like he was going to come, Zeke stopped, then slapped the clothespins until they fell off. My nipples were on fire, but I liked it. I screamed again into the briefs, then shuddered as I felt him untie my wrists. "Bend over, boy," he said. I pictured Zeke as an old man, proud silver hair, still-firm body, still-hard cock.

Then I bent over as instructed and he beat me, whipped me and spanked me. My ass burned as much as my nipples did. For a second, I flashed on our videographer friend. He sure would have enjoyed seeing this. Finally, when Zeke had had enough, he had me lie on his bed, my ankles bound, and removed the briefs. I lay on my side, my hands free as he started to fuck my face. It was a slightly awkward angle, but I didn't mind. I played with his balls and focused on keeping my lips wrapped firmly around my teeth while Zeke had his way with my mouth. That's the only way I can describe it. "Do you want my come all over you, do you want me to come on your face, you little whore?" he asked. I whimpered in agreement, and he slapped my cheeks again, each one a few times, as if somehow getting confirmation by the reddening of my skin. Then I got what he'd promised: a face full of come. He seemed to come harder than he ever had, or maybe I just noticed it more.

Then he turned sweet, soft, gentle, taking my dick between his lips and going down on me in a way he never had before, tender and careful, slow and meticulous. I had expected a rough and dirty blow job, but I got the opposite. Somehow, the contrast made tears spring to my eyes. He sucked me like he loved me. I came, spurting into his mouth, and he swallowed every drop.

We crashed hard, neither of us speaking a word about the protest except to set the alarm for 5:00 a.m., which would give us an hour before we had to leave. We showered together in the morning, and I was a little sad to leave the traces of him down the drain. We wore matching KISS ME T-shirts (the KISS THIS design, with an arrow pointing to the crotch, had been rejected by all but the guy who'd suggested it). The kiss-in was mobbed, with plenty of queer guys and girls, as well as straight couples and interested bystanders waving signs that said, FREE LOVE and EQUAL RIGHTS and WE DO and EQUAL CAMPUS FOR ALL. We had more than a thousand people, exceeding our expectations by far. Our "little" protest got written up in all the local press, and even made it onto CNN, with the focus on a kiss between Zeke and me, dubbed the "Kiss-In Organizers." I'd like to think we had a small role in getting our campus numbers up so that at the next poll, 96 percent of the student body said they supported gay marriage rights, and it was a top priority for more than 40 percent of the student body.

At one point, while doing my duty and sucking face, I looked up to see our videographer friend. He winked, then whipped out his camera. I flashed him a smile, grabbed Zeke, and helped make history.

FRAT-NAPPED

Logan Zachary

It truly wasn't my fault. I'll admit, I had two beers at the frat party, but I'm twenty. I know, but I started kindergarten late due to a Halloween birthday. For the last two years after graduation, I've bounced from job to job. This weekend, my brother Greg invited me to check out his university and see if I could meet some of the professors. Maybe get a jump on my application.

My parents wanted me to choose a major.

I wasn't even sure I wanted to go to college.

The party started out fun enough. I nursed a beer for over an hour. The last few swallows were as warm as...well, what it looked like.

The second beer went down faster with all the chips and pretzels I ate, but once I started eating the fruit, the alcohol hit me. Little did I know the fruit was spiked, and I became really tired, so I decided to go lie down on Greg's bed.

I staggered up the wooden stairway to the third floor and

found his room. I flopped down on his bed and was asleep before the dust settled.

The next thing I knew, I felt hands all over me. Something like a pillowcase was placed over my head, and a roll of duct tape screeched in protest. I was groggy; otherwise I would have said something sooner or put up more of a fight.

Something was thrown over me, and I felt my body being rolled up in it. I was lifted and carried away. I tried to escape, but my arms were pinned to my sides, and my legs were held together securely.

Wake up, wake up, I told myself. Being the center for the varsity football team, I was strong, but rolled up like an enchilada, I was helpless.

Male laughter surrounded me. Maybe Greg's frat brothers were playing a prank on me. Was I supposed to be in his room? Then the thought struck me. Even though Greg was my big bro, I was the same size. Did they think I was him?

Down several flights of stairs, the cool night air enveloped me. I heard a car door open and then I was dropped inside. The engine revved, and I was in motion. I could feel a few bodies next to me, but I couldn't speak. Whoever taped the pillowcase to my head covered my mouth too well.

We drove around for a while and then stopped. Doors opened and hands grabbed and carried me again. The next thing I knew, my arms were tied above my head, and I was dangling from something. Whatever had been wrapped around my body was gone, and I was free. Well, not quite.

The pillowcase still covered my head. A hand gently pushed me, and I swung in the air. My body spun around and around. I felt the weight of my body, pulling hard on my wrists.

Then a hand caressed my ass. It stroked one cheek and then the other. Two fingers ran down the seam of my jeans that hugged my butt. A small hole at the corner of one of my back pockets exposed my underwear. I felt a finger explore that opening and rub my briefs. The finger moved them, and then touched my bare flesh.

Excitement washed over my body. I felt a stirring in my loins. *Don't sprout a woody now,* I thought.

The finger came out of the rip, and my body spun free again. Halfway around, hands stopped me. They both touched my knees and worked their way up. The thumbs trailed along my inseam and came together at the crotch. Each thumb ran over a ball, and I could feel them lift up against my body. Semiwood was quickly hardening. My jeans were tight, and there wasn't a lot of extra room in them. If my hands had been free, I would have adjusted myself, discreetly.

As if reading my mind, a hand moved my package. I sprang to instant hard-on. The fingers outlined my cock and worked their way up. The button on my jeans tightened, but the hands opened it without a hesitation. The zipper slowly clicked down, and then my body started to buck. My legs kicked back and forth; I pulled hard on my arms and tried to raise my lower body.

But rising up only made it easier for the jeans to be slipped down in the back, exposing my underwear-clad ass. The hands pulled my jeans down, and I felt them slipping away. Once they were off, a pair of hands grabbed my right leg and another pair grabbed my left. They pulled in opposite directions, holding me spread-eagled in the air.

Another set of hands pulled up my T-shirt and traced the waistband of my Hanes.

I kicked hard with my legs, but I was held firm and fast. I felt a face press against my erection, and the hands pulled my butt forward. The hands massaged each cheek, as a tongue licked my balls through the fabric. I could feel a wet spot growing on the thin white material. How many people were watching? It felt great, but I didn't want everyone watching me get stripped.

The hands pulled the Hanes down in the back, and my smooth, bare ass was exposed. Fingers explored it, pinching and caressing, digging into the cleft.

The owners of the hands that had pulled them down touched me. A face was pressed into my ass. I could feel a nose and the chin in my crease. The hands spread my cheeks. A wet thing explored next. It licked up and down the groove and dove in deeper.

My whole body went rigid. Not there, not there, not...

And then the mouth found it and kissed my hole. It seemed to suck on it, trying to open me up. It pulled hard on me, and my body refused to move. Then the tongue stuck out and explored the hole, and my body went wild. I thrashed and jerked and floundered around.

The hands held me in place, as the tongue drove in deeper and deeper. I could feel my underwear being slipped farther down in front, as my hard-on strained to escape. How many people were watching? All guys? All girls? Was I being videotaped?

The pleasure from having my butthole licked was amazing. Was this what they meant by being rimmed?

A cold metallic feeling started at my hip and worked its way up. Snip, snip, snip, and my shirt was off in pieces. Only my underwear barely covered part of me, and the waistband was slipping.

More hands appeared, and two caressed up my sides and combed through the hair in my armpits. Sweat poured out of them as I hung helpless. The touch tickled but stimulated more than just an annoying tease.

Another pair played across my shoulders. A patch of hair

grew out of the center of my chest. The fingers combed through the tuft and gently pulled on it. They then spread out to the side and caressed my nipples. Both rose to sharp peaks under their touch. How many places in the human body caused you to feel this way?

A new face took over licking my ass. I knew it was new, because bristly hair of a moustache and beard tickled my tender hole. A closely buzzed head scrubbed my asscheeks.

The extra movement finally dislodged my underwear. My cock sprang free, fully erect and hard. It was the only thing holding my briefs in place, and now they slid down my legs. A hand pulled them off one leg, and before I could resist, they were gone. Now, I was buck-ass naked.

Free of clothes, my cock became fair game. One hand touched it lightly and ran down the underside. The nails teased my fuzzy balls and made them jump.

My cock rose up higher, as a tongue played along the underside. Flicking side to side, it worked its way slowly to the swollen tip. The mouth opened and pulled the tip inside. It closed around the end, and the tongue ran circles around it. The mouth pulled it in deeper, and a sucking pressure made my head fall back in pure pleasure. The mouth engulfed all eight inches and tickled my balls as they rested on his chin. Slowly, my cock withdrew.

"His hair tickles," a man's voice said, at my waist.

"Shave him," another man answered.

"Shave him, shave him," was chanted in the room.

I tried to cross my legs, but they were held firmly.

All was quiet for a few moments, and then I heard the sound of shaving cream coming out of the can. A foamy cream blob landed on my groin, and a hand smoothed it around my erection and down and across my balls.

"Hold very still," a husky voice commanded. "You wouldn't want me to slip."

A cold sharp edge of a razor blade touched my pelvis, right above my cock. The metallic scrap slid down to its base, removing a strip of hair along the way. Another smooth strip followed, alongside the first one. Cold metal quickly removed the hair above my penis.

The hand massaged my dangling balls and pulled one down gently. The razor shaved along one. The fingers rolled my ball as the razor did its deed. The hands moved to the other testicle and repeated the process.

A warm washcloth wiped along the inside of my leg and moved to one smooth ball. It pulled it down and moved to the other. It cleaned above my erection and moved to clean along my thick shaft. Once I'd been washed, something waved in front of me, drying me. As the water evaporated, the sensitive skin was cooled by the breeze.

Someone said, "Bong him."

I heard a few beer cans crack open, and a cold spray crossed my bare leg.

How was I going to get the bong, when my mouth was duct-taped closed?

I didn't have long to wait. A rubber tube was placed between my asscheeks. All the saliva still remained and had loosened my virgin butt. The tube slipped in easily.

"Bong him, bong him," a chant started.

Suddenly, ice cold beer filled my ass. Pressure rose as I filled up. A beer enema? How embarrassing. I couldn't just let it all go in front of everyone. More beer poured into me, and I squeezed my buttcheeks together, tighter, but the tube was still inside. I was going to burst.

"He's going to blow," someone called.

The tube was removed, and a plastic bucket was jammed against my butt, just as the pressure became unbearable. Beer flowed out of me, and my body went limp. I was so glad my face was covered.

"Bong him, bong him," the crowd started again.

A small trickle of beer ran down my legs, and I felt the tube reinserted. This time it hurt. The cold beer must have tightened my hole. The fingers found my hole and plunged in, the tube followed.

Another wave of cold beer entered me, and a few more cans were opened. My butt filled up, but this time a hand held the tube in.

"Who wants to drink first?"

The tube was adjusted, and I felt the pressure lessen.

"I'm next," someone said, and my body shifted.

"He's empty."

"Fill him up again."

Another cold wave entered me.

This time as the pressure rose, a mouth engulfed my penis. Lips slid down my length as a hot, wet tongue worked the underside. My balls bounced off his chin and swung back for more.

The pressure inside my ass pushed against my prostate.

A hand stroked my shaft as the other one played with my balls. My cock slipped in and out of his mouth, beating the back of his throat.

The orgasm hit, and I filled the willing mouth. My balls drained, my butt drained, and I was drained.

My body was overwhelmed. I couldn't focus on anything. I must have passed out, for the next thing I knew I was being lifted down. I was placed on a soft pad.

My limp body was gently rolled over. I felt my ass being raised up, and a pad was placed under my belly. Hands grabbed my ankles and spread my legs apart. My buttcheeks opened, and I heard a collective gasp.

Drops of oil fell on my bottom and trickled down my crack. It hung onto my body, being so thick. My smooth balls quickly were covered with it. Small drops fell as the amount increased. A finger ran down the crease and circled my hole. The digit explored it as the oil continued and followed the tip's trail. I could feel my opening fill with oil, and it pooled there. As the finger inserted itself, the oil flowed inside me. Another finger followed from someone else, and I could feel myself open up. More oil poured in, as the two fingers played and teased me.

My spent cock rose from the semihard state to full erection. Applause greeted it.

I felt it jerk up and down as if taking a bow.

Hands massaged my bubble butt and spread my cheeks. The fingers that were exploring left, and the thumbs of the massaging hands took their place.

I felt someone move closer behind me. The hands worked my butt, and a thick cock slipped along my buttcrack. The fat fleshy cock sandwiched between my cheeks like a brat. As the hands worked, his hips matched their rhythm.

The cock slid along me, and the tip pressed the tender spot. It teased the hole, trying to get in, but slipped across it, rubbing the meaty shaft the entire length. Heavy balls bounced against my ass and slowly rocked back and forth.

My ass begged for his entry. The penis teased and tormented me, until the hands grabbed my hip bones and posed the rigid member on target. With one swift thrust, he was inside me, to the hilt. The furry balls pressed against me, seeking entry also.

Slowly, the hard-on slid out to the mushroom head and popped out. It pressed forward and entered me again. It felt like it had swollen double in size. The thick, veined shaft filled my virgin ass. He drove into me, burying himself all the way to the base. His balls mashed against my butt.

I could feel how low they hung down my cheeks. I swore they dangled and banged against my own nut sac, furry against my newly shaved scrotum.

The pelvis drilled in and out, driving the penis in and out the full length. With each stroke, the speed and intensity increased. His balls slapped against my cheeks.

The pleasure was amazing, and I adjusted my position to enjoy it more. As I moved, my ass clamped down on the hard cock as it drove inside. His balls pulled up along my asscheeks. He pulled back and frantically entered me again, shooting a hot load inside of me.

My ass spasmed around the thick cock, sucking all the hot cum out and milking it for all it was worth. My greedy ass wanted more and tried to pull him in again.

A low moan sounded behind me as the shaft was removed.

I felt the man collapse to his knees behind me. His mouth landed on my hole and sucked on it. His tongue entered, trying to retrieve what his cock had just deposited.

I pushed my ass into his face and rode his tongue. Thick, hot fluid passed from my ass to his mouth and back. Suck and blow, suck and blow.

I wanted my arms and legs to be free so I could touch and handle all that was around me. Never had I realized my body could feel such pleasure.

As the hungry mouth finished eating, my body was moved again. This time, I found myself flat on my back. My cock sprang free and slapped against my belly.

Lying there, I waited, not sure what to expect next. A hairy leg brushed alongside my leg. I felt someone climb across my narrow hips, hands slid a condom onto my cock and a tight butt began to sit on it. The ass hung in midair for a moment, swallowed my dick and slid down along my shaft.

It didn't take long. The explosion that arose in my balls tore out of my shaft and filled the rubber. The tight ass continued to ride it. My pelvis pounded into him, as wave after wave of cum spewed out of me. My body tingled and shivered with the overload of sensation. As the last drop left my cock, my body became heavy, all energy gone, and I lay exhausted on the floor. Everything was spent from my body. I couldn't move.

Several minutes passed and gentle hands worked the tape from the pillowcase. The pressure holding my mouth closed released, and I rocked my jaw from side to side to loosen it again. The tape ripped off, and the pillowcase rose.

The bright light blinded me at first, but a smiling face greeted me. "Are you ready to apply now?" my brother Greg asked. "The brothers at the frat house would love a younger brother."

I looked around the room.

All the heads nodded in agreement.

My head joined them; it was all I could do.

When the weekend was over, I returned home, where Mom and Dad waited for me. "So? How did it go? Did Greg show you a good time?"

"He did," I said, and smiled at the memories.

"So?" Mom asked.

"I start Spring term."

Dad clasped my hand and shook it hard. "I'm proud of you, son."

"Have you decided what you'll study?" Mom asked.

I smiled. "Anatomy," I answered proudly. I couldn't wait to start my lessons.

BEN AND THE WORKOUT

Rob Wolfsham

B en Ball was a strapping young college student, twenty years old, five-nine, with a mop of black hair, shaggy sideburns, and a lean body he tried to define with tight shirts. He had a small pale face and dark eyes, and he loved working out every night at the university's recreation center.

It became a routine when the semester began. Ben had tired of being the skinny lanky kid he always had been and the way he was always made fun of in high school. He wanted muscles like the guys on sports teams and at the gym. His small frame frustrated him as it was hard to build muscle onto it.

However, a starker frustration appeared for Ben when he finally realized that he didn't want muscles just for himself, and he didn't simply admire muscles on other guys for their strength and ability. He wanted *them*. He wanted strong muscled arms to wrap around his light naked body and press him against a smooth rock-hard torso, breathing and sweating with a large reassuring hand cupping behind his head to hold him close.

Ben had found it harder and harder to contain himself when he went to the rec. He purchased extra-tight boxer briefs to stifle the constant five-inch erections that just happened to pop up whenever a well-defined frat bull walked by and worked on sculpting his body.

"Yo, Ben," one of them called to him now from where he sat at a leg curl bench, working his blond hairy tree trunks, flexing under the weights as he lifted his powerful defined legs.

Ben watched this carefully as he stood with his fifteen-pound dumbbells and worked his biceps, quickly and nervously. He watched Michael with intense satisfaction as he worked up a sweat. Michael Bowey came to the gym as regularly as Ben did. They had grown accustomed to each other's presence, each other's musk, and the banal conversations that danced around school, music and sex. Michael often spotted for Ben and liked to help the little guy work his muscles.

"Hey, Michael man, I got a question," Ben panted. "You got a girlfriend?"

Michael puffed out his cheeks and lifted an excessively large weight with his legs. He lowered it carefully to a resting position. "No."

"Oh." Ben lifted and dropped, lifted and dropped. "That's cool man."

They worked in silence for a moment, and Michael wiped his sweaty thick neck where some of his curly blond hair tickled him. "Never really something I cared about. Girls are bitches."

Ben's pulse quickened. He couldn't tell if it was from lifting or from the insatiable curiosity that piqued at the thought of why a guy like Michael didn't have a girlfriend and never cared.

"You've been working those legs for a while, man," Ben started. He dropped his arms for the last time with the weights and felt the dull soreness. He was done and placed the weights back on the rack.

"Yeah, I think I'm done too," Michael said. "I just needed to kill some frustration. I had a real awkward moment with my roommate."

"Yeah? What happened, man?"

Michael brought one of his legs up on the bench and his gym shorts slid back like curtains revealing more of his thick thighs where the blond hair darkened. "It's kind of embarrassing." He gave a short disinterested laugh. "I mean my roommate walked in on me jackin' it."

Ben laughed nervously. "Oh, shit man...that's great."

"No, it was bad!" the blond said laughing. "He didn't even get out right away. He just said 'Oh, sorry man, I just need to get something, I'll be gone in two seconds,' and then he lingered looking for something in his desk for a good thirty seconds while I'm holding my piece."

Ben looked at Michael, astonished. "Dude, when you walk in on another guy, the proper response is to just immediately bolt out the door and run away."

"Yeah, that's what I thought."

"He probably just wanted to scam on your nuts or something."

Michael laughed. "Yeah, probably, fucking fag. I didn't even get to finish."

"Aw, man, got blue balls?"

"Yeah, pretty bad. Thought I'd come here and work myself up again."

Ben looked around at the rest of the secluded workout room, taking a quick second to notice himself in the reflection of the wall mirrors. He was sweaty, red in the face, and the black stubble around his jawline and chin made him look worse, yet he was still attractive in his skinny scruffy way. He watched Michael in the reflection rubbing his legs behind him. It was almost midnight and they were alone.

"Yeah, man, I think I worked myself up too," Ben said. He turned around and watched Michael in the flesh. He was an attractive guy and Ben was noticing. A wave of panic washed over Ben and crashed down into his crotch.

Michael looked up. "What do you mean?"

Ben coughed and picked up another weight, "I mean I worked out a lot. I think I just made myself tired, man." He toyed with a ten-pound weight with his right arm.

"I thought you were done," Michael said suspiciously.

Ben looked at the weight and quickly put it back, "Yeah, no, I'm done."

Michael smirked. "Ben, what's the deal?" He brought his other leg up to the bench and the shiny blue gym shorts on that side slid back as well, revealing his thighs far down. At this point a guy would normally quickly adjust and pull the shorts back up to his knees, but instead Michael simply spread his legs just a little.

Ben was huffing now, not from exhaustion, but from Michael's inviting odor.

Michael brought a hand to his leg and tugged at some of the blond hairs. "Hah, you know, I should just take care of myself here. Why walk back to my dorm, this place is pretty much closed now."

Ben looked around the empty room full of exercise equipment. "Yeah…" he felt himself say.

"Yeah?" Michael echoed incredulously. "What, you a fag too?"

"What the fuck, man?" Ben got defensive, puffing up. "You're the one talking about beating it in here."

"Only 'cause I can tell you wanna see me do it, fag."

Ben panicked more. The word struck him. He knew he was a faggot. He wanted Michael to do it, to whip it out and stroke it, to let him stroke it, to let him suck it; grapple with him on the bench, wrap his legs around him and feel him and let him slide his cock against his asshole—

"I'm gonna do it then," Michael said. He grabbed one side of his shorts like he was going to readjust it to his knee like guys normally did, but instead pulled it back toward himself and leaned back on the inclined bench, suddenly casting fluorescent light on his hardening organ.

Ben was completely unprepared for the sight and stared rapt as Michael fondled his cock, getting himself up.

"Fuck this;" Michael said annoyed, "You should be doing this, with the way you're looking at it. Fuck, you are a faggot."

Ben didn't say anything and brushed the sweaty mop of hair aside from his brows, but it didn't help. He felt his legs move and the muscles jolt and spasm until he was stepping slowly toward Michael, falling down onto his knees before him at the bench, ready to pray.

Michael smirked and pulled his gym shorts down, lifting his ass to pull the band to his knees. "You suck too?"

Ben didn't know what else to say. "Yeah, I suck."

Michael's cock raged hard and taut now, standing at least seven inches. It was cut and throbbing, pale and traced by thick veins. Ben found his hand wrapping around it, tugging on it, until his lips closed in.

Michael sighed and pulled his sleeveless shirt up to his neck so he could rub one of the nipples on his smooth defined chest. "That's it."

Ben's lips kissed the head and he slipped farther down. It felt strange and foreign, being his first time sucking cock. The taste wasn't what he expected, just a salty skin taste. It enamored him and soon he was devouring it, shoving it back into his throat like he just discovered something new and delicious. He bobbed and weaved and swirled his tongue around the head like he'd want done to himself.

"Fuck, man," Michael crooned. "I can tell this isn't gonna last long. I might make you do it twice."

Ben grunted and jerked his head back and forth, back and forth until he plunged and buried his nose in the trimmed blond pubes with their underarm smell. He was surprisingly adept at controlling his gag reflex as the thick head slipped past his tonsils. He repeated the plunge several more times and Michael gasped and grabbed Ben's shaggy hair, forcing him back down again and again.

"You swallow? Yeah, you do, cum slut."

Ben gagged and tried to say something, everything in his throat clasping around the thick invading cock.

"Yeah, gag on that shit," Michael groaned. "Fuck."

Ben felt a change. Michael's hand shook on his head with each dive, his knuckles tightened and the grip on his hair grew painful. He knew what was happening and his heart raced and his own cock throbbed in his boxer briefs.

"Fucking swallow it," Michael barked.

Ben gagged hard when an eruption of spunk flooded his throat and Michael groaned. It came again and again in waves. Ben's gulping didn't keep up and his entire mouth filled and he had to pull off.

The sixth spurt of cum shot onto Ben's neck and cum spilled from his lips. His first instinct was to spit onto the floor.

"Yeah, that's it," Michael growled through his teeth. "Fucking cum eater." He slapped his cock against Ben's cheek with three quick taps as pearls oozed out the tip and smeared on his face.

Ben wiped his chin, satisfied and degraded.

"Clean it off." Michael grabbed his hair again.

Ben complied and put it back in, licking all around, searching for stickiness with his tongue and coaxing more cum out of the softening head.

Michael let go and Ben pulled off and rubbed his own throbbing dripping cock in his shorts, feeling like he could shoot with just a few tugs.

The blond handled his own cock for a moment, like he was inspecting the work done on it. He noticed Ben touching himself. "Yeah, take care of yourself," he said, sounding disparaging and encouraging at the same time.

Ben quickly pulled his shorts down and after a few strokes he shuddered and grabbed Michael's hairy shin with his other hand and his five inches were spewing onto the floor under the bench.

"Shit," Michael said, jerking his leg out from Ben's grip mildly disgusted. "That was fast. I got you pretty worked up, I guess."

Ben nodded and his sweaty mop of hair rattled side to side as he finished himself off. "It's sometimes a problem, man," he half laughed.

"Yeah, no shit. Thank god you don't like girls. They would laugh their asses off at you for shit like that. Hell, I'm laughing my ass off at you."

Ben reddened and hid his cock in his shorts, pulling them up. "Yeah, man," he muttered.

Michael pulled himself off the bench, standing up and readjusting his shorts. "All right, I'm jetting. You be here tomorrow night?"

It was more of a command than a question.

Ben nodded, "Yeah, man. I'll be here." He watched the tall

muscled blond grab his wallet and keys from the floor, annoyed by the spurts of cum that had come dangerously close, and then he left.

Ben rested on his knees and licked his lips, still able to taste the dry saltiness. He smirked and wiped the cum off his neck that had run in a trail down to his tight shirt. He looked at the cream in his hand and lunged for it with his tongue, devouring it. Then he fell on his hands and burrowed his face in his own cum spurts, licking them off the rubber-tiled floor, like a pig at a trough.

The door Michael had left through swung open and an old Latina lady in an orange custodian's vest entered. She stopped at the sight of Ben eating cum off the floor and shook her head. *"Ay dios mio,* not another."

THE FULL RIDE

Gavin Atlas

The disapproving look in my mother's eye was not about me leaving the house wearing next to nothing. Something bigger was bothering her.

"Christopher, I have opened the last of your college emails." She annunciated each syllable when angry.

My eyes widened. *They'd arrived?* "Shouldn't I have opened them?" It infuriated me that I'd had to give my parents my passwords in exchange for application fees.

"You did not get into Harvard, nor Yale, nor Princeton, nor Stanford, nor Swarthmore, nor Amherst, nor—"

"Okay, gosh, please stop." My heart raced. "Where *did* I get in?"

"Nowhere. You are zero for twenty." She rubbed her temples. "Your father always said you were a disappointment. This is a disaster."

My stomach felt hollow. In the back of my mind, I'd been a little afraid of this possibility, but now that it had come true, I had to fight tears. I swallowed and tried to regain my composure, reminding myself that it wasn't all my fault. My parents were impossible prestige whores who wouldn't let me apply to realistic places.

"Maybe there's still time to apply to State." *Like I had originally wanted*, I silently added.

"Your father and I will only pay for the best, Christopher. Now he might make you enlist."

Oh, my god. This was so unfair. "I understand. I'm sorry I'm such a…disappointment. I'm going to see Mr. Lazlo. He used to be a college professor. He might have some ideas."

"I wish you had spent as much time with your math tutor before the SATs," she fumed. "And why are you wearing such tiny shorts and that cut-off shirt? You look like you're for sale!"

My mom wasn't stupid. I may have had muscles and a somewhat masculine demeanor, but I did dye my hair blond and show a lot of skin. She probably knew I wanted men to notice me, but I had an excuse prepared. "Mr. Lazlo doesn't charge you for tutoring if I cut his grass. I figured you'd want me to wear old clothes."

Her mood changed slightly. "Oh, if it's free, I don't mind, although I wish you would wear something else. I hope he has the connections to get you in somewhere we approve of."

I waved over my shoulder and slipped out the back door. I walked slowly to give myself time to shake off my dejection. I wasn't sure Mr. Lazlo could help. I just wanted to see him.

"Hey, bud," Mr. Lazlo said when I arrived, his massive frame still covered in a pinstriped shirt, tie, and wool dress pants. "You look down. More calculus trouble?"

"Yes, but that's not why I'm here." I stripped off my shirt. "Right now, I really need to get fucked."

A sly grin appeared on Mr. Lazlo's face. "I hoped that was why you came over." As much as I had begged, Mr. Lazlo refused to touch me until after my eighteenth birthday, but in the two months since, he'd been inside me at least once a week. When I was a sophomore, two seniors from the soccer team gave me enough experience to know that Mr. Lazlo was an awesome top.

He unbuttoned my denim shorts, and they fell to the ground. He laughed. "No underwear! Ooh, and you've shaved your crotch. Are you using your mother's tanning bed naked? You're getting brazen, young man." He picked me up and threw me over his shoulder, spanking and groping me all the way to his bed.

In moments he had me lubed up with my legs in the air. He wanted me to practice putting condoms on him, so I'd know later in life if my partners were using them correctly, but he could tell from my moans that I was too impatient to worry about that today, so he quickly suited himself up.

He entered me slowly, and I breathed great puffs of air while my hole adjusted to the penetration.

"Ooooh, Christopher," he said. "So nice. I'm not hurting you, am I? Should I go slow?"

"No. I've been bad. My ass needs to be punished." Mr. Lazlo was never angry with me, but I loved angry sex, and he liked to role-play.

"Then you're going to be pummeled, young man, and there's nothing you can do about it."

"Oh, yes, sir," I said, moaning. I looked up at him while he fucked me, slowly increasing his pace. Mr. Lazlo was six-two and built like a bouncer. My mom said he was Hungarian and "looked like an actor on a soap opera." She flirted with him every chance she got.

Take that, Mom. He's fucking me.

I put my hands above my head, pretending Mr. Lazlo had me tied up. I'd asked him to in the past, since it was my number-one fantasy, but he'd said we weren't ready. However, keeping my hands above my body did encourage him to jerk me off. I loved that.

"I adore fucking your ass, Christopher." My tutor's breathing was ragged from shoving in and out of me. "God...your skin is so soft and your body is so beautiful."

"I've been working out every day," I boasted.

He squeezed my arm muscles without slowing his pace. "I can tell," he rasped.

"Can I tell you a secret?" Even though his thrusts made my entire body rock, I did my best to look into his dark-brown eyes.

"You'd better tell me, boy." His vise-tight grip on my nipple and pumping of my cock made me feel completely owned by his lust.

"Since I can't ever please my dad, my goal in life is to please men with my hole. Men like you."

"Oh, oh god," he said. "I see." I felt little jolts of wonderful pain as he nipped at my neck.

"Instead of going to college, I'm going to be your permanent ass slave."

"Oh...yessss," he hissed. His thrusts increased, and he began to grunt. I felt his balls slap against my buttcheeks, and each stroke hit my prostate hard. *Yep, I was too dumb for college. All I was good for was getting my ass fucked.*

Those thoughts sent me over the edge, and I shot in his hand in wave after wave. God, he was good. At the same time, Mr. Lazlo shoved in one last time, shouting "Yes...Jesus, yes!" His face was red and dripping sweat.

"Did you want me to finish fast?" he asked, wiping my come off his hand with a towel.

"I would have lasted longer if you hadn't turned me on with talk of being my slave. Why did you say your ass needed punishing anyway?"

The satisfaction I'd felt from coming drained.

"Hey, what's wrong? You look so sad." He gave my shoulder a reassuring squeeze.

"I didn't get into college. Maybe I'm bad at math, but that's not the main problem. My parents made me apply only to top schools, and they all rejected me. I feel like such a loser. If college isn't an option, maybe I'll just spend my life getting fucked. At least that makes me feel good."

Mr. Lazlo laughed. "Whoa, don't give up so easily on college, bud." Then he blinked and tilted his head. "Hmm, spend your life getting fucked, huh? You know, from our conversations it sounds like you're into all kinds of older guys, not just me. Correct?"

I felt my face flush. "You're hotter than hell, but yeah, you're right."

"Then there may be a way for you to achieve your...uh... goals while getting educated. I can help you get into a college. Fenton University in Kentucky. I used to be a professor there."

"What? Kentucky! There's no school my parents would pay for there."

Mr. Lazlo led me by the hand back to his kitchen, both of us still naked. He wanted to teach me to cook. "Your parents won't have to spend a dime. In fact, we'll tell them as little as possible, okay? I'll help you get something called a Bardache Scholarship, and you'll receive a full ride." He squeezed my ass and smiled.

After dinner, I asked Mr. Lazlo to call my parents and persuade them to let me attend this college instead of enlisting. He did, and I could hear my father grumble on speakerphone, "Who

the fuck has heard of Fenton University?" Mr. Lazlo guaranteed
I'd receive an excellent education and a tremendous amount of
attention from the faculty. Finally, when Mr. Lazlo mentioned
college would be completely free, my father spat, "At this point,
I don't care what the hell he does as long as it costs me nothing."
His attitude hurt me, and Mr. Lazlo sensed it. He spent an hour
holding me and stroking my hair.

My nerves were rattled. Mr. Lazlo drove me to Kentucky to
meet with an admissions officer named Martin Kelly. I'd asked
Mr. Lazlo why he thought I had a shot at Fenton.

He gave me a big grin. "You'll see."

Mr. Lazlo dropped me off and told me to meet him in the
cafeteria later. While walking to the admissions department, I
noticed the buildings. Lots of impressive red-brick edifices with
white columns along a well-manicured quad. It seemed digni-
fied, for sure.

When I entered Mr. Kelly's office alone, he looked me up
and down, but quickly turned away as if something about me
annoyed him. I was surprised by how short he was, and I'm not
a tall guy myself. He had a pale complexion and the nervous
air of someone busy and distracted. He frowned as he perused
my file.

"I'm not sure why Mr. Lazlo asked me to waive the application deadline for you. Your achievements are mostly impressive, but with that math score, you're not qualified for Fenton.
I'm sorry." Mr. Kelly fidgeted in his chair. He actually did look
sorry.

"It's okay," I said, my heart in my shoes. "It figures something as incredible as this Bardache Scholarship would go to
someone with a better record."

"What?" Mr. Kelly sat up straight and looked at me in

amazement. "Well now, that makes all the difference! I had no idea you were interested—oh, here it is in Lazlo's note. I thought he was just tormenting me by sending such a hot boy, but he's not. What are you doing with your clothes on? Get naked, get on my desk, and put your legs in the air!" Mr. Kelly turned the envelope Mr. Lazlo's recommendation had come in upside down, and a condom and sample pack of lube spilled out.

"Ex-excuse me?" I couldn't believe what I was hearing. "I have to let you fuck me to get into college?" My dick instantly hardened.

Mr. Kelly scurried to clear off his desk. "If you're interested in a Bardache."

It all fell into place. This is what Mr. Lazlo meant when he said I could combine my goals with an education. *Holy shit.* Mr. Kelly gave me an impatient look. I couldn't believe I wanted to go along with this, but I found myself pulling off my shirt and pants. I didn't understand myself. Why did I want this kind of humiliation?

"You're absolutely gorgeous." Mr. Kelly ogled my naked body. "You could be in porn," he whispered as he fondled my ass. "Get on up there."

My heart pounded as I mounted the desk. I was still stunned. I had to give up my ass to get into college! My body hummed with excitement I could feel from my stomach to my teeth.

He stripped as fast as he could. He had a pudgy, hairy body— the opposite of Mr. Lazlo's, except that Mr. Kelly also had a large and very hard dick. That's what counted most.

The desk was low. Perhaps Mr. Kelly had requested this desk on purpose as it was the perfect height for him to fuck my ass.

I still needed to understand. "So everyone else admitted gets in because of their brains, but I have to give up my hole to you?"

"That's exactly right." His confirmation made me moan. As he barreled into me, I gasped. The invasion had me reeling in heated but fantastic shame.

He reamed me as hard as he could, but he suppressed his grunts and groans, probably so his coworkers in nearby offices wouldn't hear. His dick was too large for me to stay silent, however, and before long, he'd stuffed my underwear in my mouth to keep me quiet. I bit down on the white cloth to help me make it through his vicious pounding. I let him ravish me, offering myself up as if my future depended on it. Less than ten minutes later, he peaked and shot his load deep inside me. He couldn't help himself and grunted so loud it was practically a roar. That turned me on so much that I came as well, shooting up to my chest and shoulder.

"We haven't had a Bardache Scholar in years. Are you always this easy a bottom? And this good?"

"Yes, sir," I said, panting. "My ass is yours whenever you want."

"Welcome to Fenton University, Christopher."

My parents allowed me to attend Fenton only after the university gave me a stipend on top of the scholarship. Again, Mr. Lazlo had to drive me to campus. My mother barely waved good-bye, and my father had a lunch he "couldn't miss." On the other hand, I almost cried when I said farewell to Mr. Lazlo. He told me he'd visit often.

I figured that getting fucked once wouldn't be enough to pay for four years of college. Thus, I knew Mr. Kelly would be inside me often. But I was shocked when he told me that each semester it would be my responsibility to get fucked by some, possibly all, of my professors. I should have realized the Bardache Scholarship wasn't officially school sanctioned and was funded secretly by participating faculty. Mr. Kelly told me to tell no one. I'd already mentioned that I'd won a scholarship to friends and family, but he didn't have to worry about me disclosing the details. I was too embarrassed.

There was one drawback: I couldn't choose my own classes. Mr. Kelly acted as my advisor, handpicking my courses to satisfy my graduate requirements as well as satisfy the needs of my many "masters." Also, I wasn't allowed to make passes at teachers in case they weren't "part of the program." My predicament stunned and excited me. How many men would I have to bottom for during my college career?

For the first week, I went to every lecture with an erection, wondering which of my professors would be in my ass. I was attracted to all of them. My econ prof, Dr. Bellamy, looked like he'd been a linebacker in college. My Spanish professor, Señor Vargas, was a dashing gray-haired god from Venezuela. Calculus, which I couldn't believe I had to take again, was made less insufferable by Professor Landon, a handsome and amiable bearded bear. But the one who intrigued me the most was Professor Archer, my English instructor. He was short, almost as short as Mr. Kelly, and he was African-American, or more accurately, African-Caribbean, as he was from Saint Lucia. Even behind his little round glasses, I could tell he had beautiful eyelashes, and he wore thick, soft-looking cable-knit sweaters that made me want to snuggle him. His demeanor, however, let me know he was more of a drill sergeant than a cuddly professor. His angry eyes bored into any students who dared to be late, and he shouted corrections along with barbed criticism every time a classmate committed a grammar infraction during an oral presentation. I didn't know what was wrong with me, but his fury made me hard.

My first paper was on Adrienne Rich's "Aunt Jennifer's

Tigers," and it received a big red *F.* There was a note: *See me today. End of office hours.*

I showed up precisely on time, but he seemed to be waiting for me impatiently.

"Christopher! You're not fulfilling the requirements of a Bardache Scholar." He closed the door behind me.

"I'm...I'm not?"

"You should be reporting to my office at least once a week."

"But I didn't know you were part of the program." So far the only person I saw regularly was Mr. Kelly. I had been assigned a single room, and I suspected the reason behind that was so Mr. Kelly had a place to screw me besides his office.

"That's no excuse. Take off your clothes."

It still felt surreal that I'd agreed to such a deal, but I shook off my disbelief and stripped. Before I could finish, he impatiently yanked down my underwear and grabbed my ass.

"Excellent firmness," he said. "Very beautiful buttocks. Bend over the desk." I did so. My dick stiffened as I expected to be lubed up and penetrated. The first crack of his hand on my buttocks shocked me. I gasped as warmth and pain radiated through my rump. He groped and squeezed my ass with strong hands, creating a delicious ache in my groin.

"What a hot boy," he murmured. Then he resumed punishing me, the blows raining down in quick succession, drawing an involuntary response from me. I moaned helplessly.

He beat me with his bare hand for several minutes. After, my ass throbbed with stinging soreness and heat, and he bent down and blew cool air on my butt. He kissed the rise of my cheeks, the contact causing me to jerk away.

He spun me around and pressed on my shoulder until I was on my knees, my face in front of his erect cock. He was as big as Mr. Kelly. Was it a requirement to have a large dick to be on staff at Fenton?

He pressed against my lips, and I opened my mouth to accept him. I had much less experience with oral sex than being fucked, but I knew to open wide enough so my teeth wouldn't graze him. He seemed to know I wasn't an expert and stayed still, letting me adapt to his girth by moving my mouth back and forth down his shaft. He tasted of warm salt, and I sucked eagerly to show him I deserved my scholarship. I was rewarded by a noticeable lengthening of his dick.

"That's good. That's enough," he said sharply. "I want to come in your ass, not your mouth." Mr. Kelly had told me I was to carry lube and condoms with me at all times. I produced them from my backpack without rising from my knees. With the practice I had during the summer with Mr. Lazlo, I was able to skillfully sheath my professor in latex while keeping him hard by kissing and fondling the shaft.

He pushed me back to lie supine on the floor, massaging my hole patiently with a generous amount of lube. "I can tell you like my dick, but look me in the eyes while I'm inside you."

I did as I was told, and he watched my expression while he guided his penis into me. When he succeeded, he gave me a very pretty smile. He seemed entirely different than the martinet he'd been during class or during my spanking. It made me happy that I'd earned kindness from him. He thrust in slowly with one hand caressing my brow and cheek.

"Mmm," he purred. "You are a very good bottom. Mr. Kelly chose well."

"Thank you, Professor Archer." I moaned and spread my legs as wide as I could to allow him total access.

"Do you know you are an *eromenos* instead of a bardache?"

"A what? I thought the scholarship was named after a guy. Joe Bardache or whomever."

"No." He licked my nipple while keeping up his slow thrusting. "'*Bardache*'...is French for bottom boy, unnhh...or young male prostitute... From, unnh...the Arabic *'bardaj'* meaning 'slave.'"

My eyes widened in alarm. "Bardache means *that*?"

"Yes," he said, nipping at my neck. "But an *eromenos* is not just fucked, but cared for and educated. It's a Greek term." His thrusts began to speed up. "I'm sorry, but this ass feels so good. I wanted to be a patient lover, but I can no longer hold back. I must ravish you with abandon. Do you mind?"

"Not at all, sir."

I gasped as he began nailing my hole in earnest. He no longer looked me in the eye but watched his dick slam into me. I rolled back farther to make myself more available and vulnerable. He growled in appreciation.

The smacking of his body against mine was almost as loud as the spanking had been. Each thrust in was so huge it pushed me backward across the hard floor until my head began to bump the wall. That didn't stop him. Soon his thrusts were so strong and deep that I was nearly shouting. If there were people in the adjoining offices, there was no way they wouldn't have heard. I was still in shock that anyone I'd told I was a Bardache Scholar—my friends, my parents—could know I was an ass slave simply by looking in a French dictionary. That humiliation combined with Professor Archer's incredible assault made me climax so hard that I shot come up to my chin. Professor Archer pushed in to the hilt, bellowing and grunting as he came inside me.

As his orgasm subsided, he bent down and kissed me fiercely. "I should have taken Kelly at his word," he said, still breathing hard. "He told me it was impossible to stay quiet while screwing you. How did you get to be such a talented bottom at such a young age?"

"I just love getting fucked."

"And I already know I love fucking you, but Christopher, the way you move beneath me, the way you spread your legs so wide, you're letting your top know that you want to be treated like a whore. In addition to composition, perhaps I need to show you how to respect yourself."

"Nah, I want to be nailed," I said.

Professor Archer gave me a thoughtful look and then nodded. "Very well, then. Let's discuss your Adrienne Rich paper. Truthfully, instead of an *F,* you deserved a *B*-plus. Let's review your arguments, and perhaps when you submit the Derek Walcott paper, you'll earn an *A.*"

I learned that my father had dug through my room at home and discovered a porn magazine. It hurt that Dad had another reason to dislike me, but at least I no longer had to hide. However, now I wasn't invited home for the holidays. My mom assured me my father would get over it "eventually," but I didn't know what I'd do until then. I had made a few friends within the school's gay alliance, but I felt shy around them as several wanted sex from me or more. I didn't want to hurt anyone's feelings by telling them I wanted daddies, so I laid low.

It seemed all my teachers gave me extra attention, but Professor Landon was the next to let me know I was to give up my ass to him, and I loved pleasing the huge and hairy instructor. While I admired the lean frame of Professor Archer, seeing Professor Landon's big belly made me just as horny. However, as much as I wanted him inside me, he spent a lot more time tutoring than fucking. The day I found out I wasn't invited home, he'd sat me down in his office and told me we had to have a talk.

"Gosh, it's bad news, isn't it? I've already had some." I explained what my father had decided.

"Oh, Christopher," he said in a soothing voice. "I'm so sorry. You know, of course, you can spend the holidays with me."

As Professor Landon put his arm around my shoulder, my mood lightened. My professors were so nice to me.

"But...you said there's something you need to talk about?"

"I never want to give up on a student, Christopher, and I know from the amount of time I'm spending with you that you're trying your best. However, I can't give you a grade higher than you're earning. And so far, you're getting a C. If you want to drop for the sake of your GPA, I'd understand."

I sighed. "Am I dumber than other Bardache Scholars? Am I a disappointment to you?"

Professor Landon's eyes softened, and he rubbed my stomach through my cotton T-shirt. "No, buddy, you please me in every way you can, and I've seen you try your hardest. It's not fair to you to have to take a class you'd never dream of signing up for simply because I'm a Bardache mentor."

"I don't want to lose you as a teacher! I promise I'm doing better in math than before. Maybe I need to give you more than I have been since you have to spend so much time tutoring me." I hastily stood up to strip. Mr. Kelly had told me to make my ass as easily accessible as possible, so now I always wore dorm shorts that could be tugged off with one pull and no underwear. Bare-assed, I leaned over Professor Landon's desk and arched my rump.

Professor Landon gave a big laugh and caressed my rear. "You certainly were the right choice for this scholarship. I've never met such a horny little bottom."

"Yes, sir. I'm here to serve."

He pulled my shorts back up. "I tell you what. You're doing

plenty to justify your scholarship, but if you want extra credit, you can earn some tonight." He wrote down an address and patted my butt. "Come by my house, and we'll try to satisfy your apparently bottomless need to bottom. For now, keep your pants on and solve these equations."

A few hours later a cab dropped me off at Professor Landon's house, and when he let me in, I did a double take. He was dressed in full leather gear.

"Strip off your clothes, handsome, and leave them in the foyer." I was nude in moments and he led me upstairs to his bedroom. It was lit by candles. I shivered with pleasure when I saw ropes attached to each bedpost.

"Lie down, Christopher," Professor Landon commanded. I did and then lifted my legs. He tied them so my ankles were suspended in midair. I was helpless to stop him from fucking me.

He lubed me up and then entered me roughly. I tried to welcome him inside by arching up to meet his thrust, but with my legs tied, the control was all his.

I was startled by a knock on his bedroom door.

"Come in!" Professor Landon yelled. Mr. Kelly and Professor Archer walked in, naked. Behind them were Dr. Bellamy and Professor Vargas! Oh, my god! I was going to get gang-banged! I was lightheaded with ecstatic need.

"You needed a treat after what your parents pulled," Professor Landon said.

"Tonight you'll show us how completely worthy you are of the full ride Fenton University is giving you," Mr. Kelly said as Professor Landon pulled out of my ass to let Professor Vargas have a turn.

As usual, Mr. Kelly managed to make me feel shame mixed with pleasure. He always reminded me I got into college because I gave him my hole. But as I felt the amazing ache of being stretched by Professor Vargas, I told myself I was receiving an honest-to-god education, and I'd done it without a cent from my damn dad. Now that I considered it, these men and Mr. Lazlo took better care of me than my father did. As Professor Vargas ground into me feverishly, I thought, I was the luckiest college boy alive.

RIGHT WAY, WRONG WAY

H. L. Champa

Y ou don't really believe that, do you?"

I snapped my head up and looked straight into Brian's eyes. He was smirking, just like always; his chin tilted up in defiance. I sighed, unable to hold in my emotions. Every day it was the same thing: another challenge, another provocation. The class was supposed to be a discussion of modern American politics. But, it had turned into a nonstop argument with Brian. I should have seen it coming. It was obvious from the minute he walked into the room on the first day.

While the rest of the kids dutifully took notes, nodding along with my every word, Brian never let a word go by without a fight. I tried to hide my worldview from the class, but my left-wing leanings were hard to keep under wraps. Brian was a Republican, a fact he wore like a badge of honor. He acted like he was cavorting with the enemy, and he never missed a chance to prove his mettle. In addition to his opinionated nature, he was cute. And, he knew it. He possessed the confidence and swagger that only came with being really good looking. Rumors about his conquests swirled all over campus. Even the faculty talked about him. Being attracted to him only made his words more infuriating.

"Actually, Brian, I do."

"That figures. Bleeding hearts are so typical."

"You consider me a bleeding heart for wanting everyone in this country to have health care?"

"Hell, yeah. I mean, if you can't afford it, get a better job. Rely on yourself, not the government. That's the way it should be."

"Brian, you know very well life isn't that simple."

"Well, it should be."

The rest of the class sat watching, their heads moving between us like they were at a tennis match. The tension in the room crackled. I loosened my tie, trying to ease the heat rising up to my face. I refused to let the guy get to me. He was older than the others by a few years; a nontraditional student. But, unlike most nontrads, Brian wasn't trying to be the teacher's pet and impress me. He seemed to enjoy trying to wind me up, getting off on making me look foolish.

"Well, Brian, I guess we'll have to agree to disagree because we're out of time. Okay, for next time, everyone please bring your essays. Have a good weekend."

The good little students shuffled along, but Brian packed his bag slowly, leaning back in his chair still watching me. I put my papers into my briefcase, unwilling to get into another discussion with Brian, but he clearly wasn't done. As I started to walk out, Brian turned his chair in my path.

"Professor Davis, you're not angry are you? Because you seem like you're pissed at me again."

"Brian, it's really not a big deal. Everyone is entitled to his opinion."

"But, you think I'm a right-wing nut, don't you?"

"I wouldn't say it that way."

"Then, how would you say it? Come on, I know it kills you."

"What kills me?"

"That you can't just scream at me like you want to. If I were you, I'd just haul off and yell, put me in my place. But, you can't, can you? Professors can't talk to students like that."

"Even if they could, that's not my style anyway."

Brian stood up, his body closer to mine than it should have been. His sandy brown hair hung over his painfully blue eyes, that smirk back on his lips. Those lips taunted me in more ways than one. Part of me wanted to smack them, the other part wanted to taste them.

"I'm not surprised."

"What is that supposed to mean?"

"Nothing. I'm just saying, in my experience, most liberals are afraid of a good fight. You seem to be no different."

"You know, Brian, just because I don't get in your face, doesn't mean I don't believe what I'm saying. I don't have to beat people up to get my point across."

"Don't you ever get frustrated? Come on, what would it hurt if you cut loose, just once?"

"I've never really thought about it, Brian."

"That's too bad. It can be so much fun."

He inched a little closer, looking into my eyes. For a moment, I felt small. He only had a few inches on me, but his presence loomed large. I swallowed hard, trying to stay calm. My palms were sweaty, but I stayed still. I didn't speak, afraid my voice would betray my frustrations. At last, Brian eased back and time started again.

"Have a good weekend, Professor Davis."

He turned on his heel and walked out without another word.

I came to class after the weekend determined to ignore Brian's attempts to bait me. I had planned a lesson to avoid the mine-fields, but when another student brought up gun control, all hell broke loose.

"Professor Davis, I imagine you are in favor of banning assault weapons?"

Brian's voice rang through the classroom; his casual arro-gance hit me like a brick wall. I cleared my throat, determined to stay calm and easy.

"As a matter of fact, Brian, I am. But we're not talking about that today. Now, if we could get back to the topic, please."

"Why don't you want to talk about it, Professor? Afraid of the truth?"

"And what would the truth be, Brian?"

"The truth is that guns are a fundamental part of our society and people who want to ban them are un-American. It's as simple as that."

"Brian, nothing is that simple. I appreciate your black-and-white view of the world, but most of the time, you'll find things are more complicated in the real world."

"It's funny that you mention the real world, Professor Davis. Considering that you don't live in it."

My temperature was rising and I could feel my face getting red. My attempts to put the argument to bed were failing. Brian was smirking happily while I tried to keep my voice steady.

"Brian, I assure you, I live in the real world."

"Not really, Professor. I mean, academia isn't exactly the real world. You sit here and spout your theories while the rest of us deal with real life. I appreciate your point of view, but it's not very realistic."

He smiled as he mocked me; the rest of the class sat silent and stunned. I felt myself shaking; my fists opened and closed slowly.

I didn't know what to say; I was too angry to react. The class sat and stared, waiting for me to continue. But I couldn't.

"Um, I'm sorry everyone, I'm going to have to cut class short today. I'm afraid I'm not feeling well. I'll see you all on Thursday."

I walked out of the room, leaving the class buzzing and murmuring about my departure. It was all I could do to get to my office and close the door. Throwing the door closed, I hurled my briefcase against the wall. I couldn't breathe. I had never been so angry in my life, and there was nothing I could do about it. Brian had gotten his way. He found his way under my skin and forced me from my own classroom. Now everything would be different. My head was in my hands when there was a knock on the door. Before I could say a word, the door opened and I saw Brian's face. A fresh batch of anger welled up inside me.

"Professor Davis, are you okay?"

"Brian, please go away."

He didn't go away. He came in and sat down in the chair across from me. The same arrogance I saw in the classroom had followed him to the office.

"I guess I really upset you, didn't I?"

He was proud. His eyes shined as he shifted in his seat, an air of satisfaction hung around him. It made me furious. I got up, pulling open the door.

"Brian, I want you to leave."

He pushed out of the chair and swaggered over to me. His hand rested against the wall, hemming me in.

"I don't think you want me to go. Not until you've had your chance to tell me off."

"Brian, I want you to leave, right now."

He pushed the door closed, my hand unable to hold it open anymore. My body was tightly coiled, but I felt paralyzed. The full length of his body pushed against mine, his knee pushing my thighs apart. His eyes crinkled at the corners, and I watched that smirk spread across his face. My fury boiled over and I pushed Brian back with both hands. He laughed as he used my desk to stop his momentum.

"That's what I've been waiting for. Get angry, Professor."

"Get the fuck out of my office, Brian."

But he didn't leave. Again he moved into my space, edging too close for comfort. This time I didn't let him dictate the terms. I started moving forward, walking him toward the door without laying a finger on him. His back hit the door, and suddenly the smile dropped from his face.

"I really got to you, didn't I, Professor?"

"You are such an arrogant bastard. You really think that your opinions matter? You're just a dumb kid."

"I'm not a kid."

"Yeah, you are. Just because you are a few years older doesn't make you any wiser."

"I'm smarter than these kids."

"No, you're louder. There's a difference. Being a smartass only works when you're smart. Regurgitating Rush Limbaugh doesn't make you learned. Get your own opinions, live a little and then get back to me."

"Fuck you, Professor."

"Fuck you too, Brian."

It was his turn to seethe. Clearly, no one had ever challenged him before, but he seemed to like it. I waited for his retort, for him to wow me with some bullshit like always. But, he didn't. Instead, his hand reached out and his fingers started to open the buttons of my shirt.

"Getting angry feels good, doesn't it, Professor?"

My shirt was open and Brian's hand pressed firmly against

my chest. My heart was pounding, my pulse echoing in my cock. It stirred even more when Brian started to open my belt. Letting him push my pants to the floor, I watched impassively as he dropped to his knees in front of me.

"I've wanted to do this since the first day of class, Professor."

"What would your right-wing buddies say if they could see you now?"

He didn't speak. His mouth closed over my cock; the warm sweep of his tongue circled the head. I thought briefly of stopping him, of letting reason take over. But listening to him groan around my cock took those thoughts out of my head.

He kept pushing me deeper into his mouth, the back of his throat touching the tip on each pass. I heard him unzip his pants, and I looked down and saw his hand pumping on his hard cock. I saw the swollen tip disappear into his fist, and I couldn't stop the moan from leaving the back of my throat. I watched his mouth and those lips work over my cock, teasing me right up to the edge. My anger was washing away, replaced by pure desire and need. As much as I wanted to come in his opinionated mouth, I had other plans.

"Stand up."

Reluctantly, he released my cock from his mouth. I pulled his T-shirt over his head, revealing the muscled chest I had longed to look at. He was self-satisfied, my admiration giving his ego a little kick. I pushed him forward over my desk, knocking the little smile right off his face. Suddenly, I was bold, my anger channeling into putting Brian in his place.

"Keep playing with that cock, Brian."

Digging in my desk, I found the bottle of lube I had hidden there years ago. I never thought I'd ever use it; it was more wishful thinking than anything else. I lubed up my fingers, pausing to stare at Brian's perfect ass for one second before I pulled his cheeks apart. My fingers pressed against his tight hole, a tiny groan coming from his mouth. I teased him for a bit, waiting until he relaxed enough for me to ease the tip of my index finger inside him. His fist stopped moving, his hips pushing back against my probing finger. I watched with deep satisfaction as Brian wiggled his hips back against my hand. For the first time ever, I saw him helpless, completely out of his element. It made my cock impossibly hard. One, two, three fingers filled his tight ass, his moans growing louder and longer with each thrust.

"You wanna get fucked, don't you?"

"Yes, Professor. Yes. Fuck me."

"Not so tough now, are you?"

He didn't respond, except to whimper as my fingers slid out of his ass. I rolled my condom on slowly, again watching Brian move his ass back toward me, eager for my cock. I held his hips, stopping his movement. His hand gripped the desk, papers crinkling and sliding underneath him. As I slid the tip over his puckered ass, I let myself smirk a little. I moved slowly as I entered him, enjoying the tight grip on my cock.

Brian turned to look at me, his face transformed into something I didn't recognize. His arrogance and hubris was all gone. If I had my way, I would fuck it right out of him. With each hard push, my anger melted. Frustration was replaced with pleasure. I kept pounding him harder and harder, unable to control myself any more. His hand sped up on his cock, stroking himself in time to my thrusts.

"Fuck, I'm gonna come."

His voice sounded weak, timid. I loved it. I was barely moving, Brian fucking backed against me with abandon. Holding his hips, I just watched my cock moving inside him. His forehead dug into my desk, his voice cracking as he came into his hand. Taking back control, I rammed my cock inside him, all my feelings cracking and breaking free. When I came, I nearly screamed, releasing days and weeks of pent-up rage and desire. I fucked him until I couldn't move anymore, collapsing against him in exhaustion.

Peeling myself from Brian's sweaty body, I sank back into my chair. Tossing the condom into the trash, I watched him straighten himself up, his façade slowly coming back to the fore.

"Professor, I'd appreciate it if this could stay between us."

"Come on, don't you want everyone to know that you got fucked by a dirty liberal?"

"I have a reputation to protect."

He leaned down and kissed me, startling me with the gesture. He walked out, back to his old self. The moment had passed as quickly as it had appeared. I picked up his essay from my desk. It was slightly crumpled but still readable. I laughed when I saw the title.

How to Learn from a Liberal.

BROTHER FOR BROTHER

Jamie Freeman

March 15, 2024

A s the limo pulls into the drive on the far side of the Grayson
Building, I can hear my driver talking into his headset. After
the first assassination attempt I had been offered an HS protec-
tion detail; after the second attempt killed my private secretary
and two legislative aides, I had no choice. For a Homeland Security goon, Charlie isn't bad. We've been together for a month
and so far, he lets me strike out on my own once in a while.
He's been more discreet than some I've heard about, giving me
enough room to play my occasional games without calling in the
DAF or the Federal Police.

"Senator Walker, you're about an hour early for the meeting,
but the Feds have swept the campus and secured the perimeter,
so you've been cleared for walkabout."

"Thanks, Charlie," I say. "See you at Grayson 10-203 in say,
forty-five minutes?"

"Right, Boss."

I step out onto the dry brown lawn and slide my shades across my eyes. The campus has changed dramatically in the past twenty years, but it's nothing I haven't seen all over the country since the wars started. High concrete barriers have been installed in front of all of the buildings, the windows dark and dense with UV and anti-EMP shielding. The central quad, once a broad grass-covered space dotted with trees, has been bricked over with an interlocking pattern of multicolored red, brown and gray stone, populated by tables and benches.

Despite the sweltering heat there are students clustered here and there studying, laughing, eating under the shade of large permanent canvas tents that sag under the weight of the still air. At the far end of the quad a single male figure reclines on a broad cement slab, muscular upper body recklessly exposed to the ozone-depleted sky.

I walk across the quad remembering my years here, when the grass still grew, the trees still cast their cool shade and our perimeters were still undefined, undefended and unlimited.

My first three years here were mostly lost in a haze of alcohol and sex, but somehow I managed to pass enough of my courses to keep myself from getting booted out, and more importantly, I joined a notoriously exclusive fraternity. As a third generation legacy whose family endowed the newly constructed frat house you might say I was destined to become an Alpha Beta. At this particular school, the brothers were a motley assortment of rich boys, the sons of the Washington A-List, congressmen, cabinet members, and even a Supreme Court Justice.

Our motto, "Brother for Brother" was something we took seriously because we knew it was the key to our privilege. Exclusivity was the only way to keep all that lovely money in the right hands.

By my senior year, I had assumed an informal leadership role in the Alpha Betas, the quiet connected son of the aristocracy to whom the nominal, "elected" leadership deferred. My family was uniquely positioned to benefit from the newly installed president (Uncle George), my parents and grandparents actively overseeing vast fortunes anchored securely in oil refineries, biotech labs, defense contractors, surveillance technologies and media concerns. Despite being positioned for greatness, like my dear uncle before me I had little interest in anything more than drugs, sex, and alcohol. I was a spoiled punk who only graduated because of my sizeable family endowments. I managed to get a lot of mileage out of the Walker Library and the Barrow-Walker School of Business despite my notoriously bad grades and continual clashes with campus security.

By the end of my first semester, I had moved into the frat house and was reluctantly sharing a two-bedroom suite with a roommate named Kyle. From the first day we met, Kyle had always wandered around our suite at all hours of the day and night stark naked, arms flexing his free weights. My first few weeks I had been insanely distracted by his strutting displays, but by midterm he and I had come to an arrangement involving some mutual cocksucking that eased the tension considerably. "Brother for brother," he said the first time he sat on the bed before me and slid my shorts down to my ankles.

The frat house, perhaps because of its sense of security and isolation, or perhaps because of the ready access to cash, drugs, alcohol and beautiful boys and girls, was rife with sexual possibilities that Kyle and I went on to exploit to the utmost during those last chaotic years of the republic. Although we were less than five miles from the capitol, we had little understanding of, or interest in, the changes that were taking place so close to our little enclave. For four years I lived in luxury and splendid isolation while the republic died less than a mile away.

As I reach the far end of the quad, I approach the reclining muscle boy, our eyes locking as I ascend the steps next to his perch. His head rolls indolently in my direction, tongue sliding wetly across his upper lip, a single finger stroking the soft treasure trail that descends from his navel into his camo pants. The movements are languid and subtle, almost as if he is moving unconsciously, but the eyes send me a clear message. I raise an eyebrow as I hit the first step and the slightest edge of a smile curls along his thick lips in response. As I reach out and lightly tap the iron banister and continue up the steps, I see the Alpha Beta tattoo, tiny red and blue letters inked just above the waistline of his left hip. The muscle below the letters ripples as I pass and the boy sits up in a fluid motion. I am past him in an instant, continuing up the steps in the direction of the side door of the Barrow-Walker Center.

I continue to walk at a steady clip, not wanting to be seen looking back at the boy by the security cams mounted on every building.

I card into the building and walk toward the central lobby and stairs. I listen for the sound of the door closing behind me, but at the instant when I expect to hear the latch clicking into place, I hear nothing. I glance back. The boy has on a tight yellow Department of American Families T-shirt now, his muscular frame shifting beneath the stylized image of four figures—two adults, two children, two male and two female—holding hands across his chest. He nods a fraction and hoists his pack onto his shoulders. An iPod implant flashes like jewelry in his right ear as he cuts left and pushes through a door into the stairwell.

I face forward, but don't look back again. I am rehearsing what I will say if I am questioned about being in the building—nostalgia, checking on the family endowment, looking for an old professor. When I reach the cool lobby I walk around the information terminals and down a short hall to the central stairwell, stopping to read messages on the bulletin-vids, taking a few sips of water to soothe my dry lips. I open the door and head down the stairs, realizing where the muscle boy has probably gone.

The overhead lights on the ground floor are at half capacity, the corridor, not currently scheduled for use, has dimmed to energy-save mode. When I reach the main hall, I see a lit doorway at the far end of the corridor where I know the faculty men's room used to be.

I push open the outer door and the scraping sound of shabby wood and aluminum against the cool marble brings back a rush of memories. So many afternoons spent under the humming fluorescent lights reading paperback porn and waiting for the occasional visitor, watching for the secret signs and sometimes falling on my knees to suck a thick cock through one of the glory holes. The outer room is largely unchanged; the walls might be lighter in color, the sinks updated, but the lights still hum, filling the silence with a droning electronic buzz that puts me on edge. My mouth is dry and my palms are sweating as I push open the second door and walk into the inner room where a row of urinals line one wall with a line of stalls opposite them. The old stalls have been replaced by full cubicles, the walls extending from floor to ceiling with no enticing gaps beneath them. All of the doors are closed except for one near the far end.

I approach the door and push it open as if I am unaware that he is there. He turns around in the small space, his cock in his hand as if he has been pissing, eyes wide in mock surprise.

"You startled me," he says calmly, although his motion was too fluid, too aware.

"Oh, sorry," I say, looking him up and down, but not moving backward.

His cock is thick and partially erect in his hand, still held firmly between us.

I look into his eyes, bright blue with dark, too-wide pupils. He is tripping on something, his iPod probably providing a musical soundtrack beneath the sound of our voices.

"So," he says, finger rubbing gently along the length of his shaft, the same finger that traced his treasure trail outside.

"DAF?" I ask, pointing at the logo on his T-shirt.

"Joke," he says, grinning and allowing his fingers to slide more boldly up and down his cock. His cock is growing quickly, the well-shaped head swelling out from beneath the cowl of a thick, dark foreskin.

"Of course," I say.

"So, Senator, you gonna close the door behind you or we gonna get busted by some fucking DAF snitch?"

I grin broadly, relieved somehow that he knows who I am, though I should probably be terrified. But fuck, if I'm going to be arrested on a morals charge, it might as well be over this boy. I step forward and pull the door closed behind me and in an instant we are all over each other, my fingers pushing his shirt up and over his head. His chest and stomach muscles are solid and hot to the touch, like heated marble. He reaches out to loosen my tie, fingers fumbling down the center of my broad solid chest, unbuttoning each white button in quick, deft motions. He pushes my oxford aside and slides the undershirt up to reveal close-cropped fur over muscle.

His hands are against my chest, their smooth heat pushing my jacket back over my shoulders, then sliding against my pecs, long manicured fingers brushing against my nipples like the fingers of a blind man reading the Braille of my desire. He pinches my left nipple and twists until he forces the air out of my lungs in a gasp, then leans forward and kisses me hard, lips hungry and insistent against mine. He pushes his solid body against me, his erection now full between us, competing with my own imprisoned cock for attention.

His tongue probes my mouth, sliding along the inside of my teeth, along the rise of my own tongue. His hands tug at the ironed cotton of my shirttail, pulling it out of my pants, fumbling with my belt buckle, the button, and the zipper. In a moment he has his hands inside the elastic band of my underwear and is stroking my cock with his long cool fingers. He never lets his mouth leave mine, lips holding me in place, pushing against me with an urgency that brings the heat of blood to my cheeks, my neck and my face.

He pushes my underwear down with a swift movement and he pulls his mouth away from me for the first time, looking quickly into my eyes, shooting me a quick smile then kissing his way across my chin, down my neck and into the fur of my chest. His mouth lingers, sucks and teases my nipples long enough for them to harden, then he bites down hard on the right nipple, forcing another surprised gasp out of me that rises into the hum of the lights, followed by the quick exhalation of a laugh that trails off in surprise.

He slides down below my nipples across the light ridges of my stomach to the narrow flat plain between my waist and the base of my now fully erect cock. As he licks and teases his way around the base of my cock, I feel the sandpaper of his stubbled chin sliding against the soft skin of my shaft. His fingers lightly stroke my balls, then trail so lightly across my thighs that they raise great swathes of goose bumps in their wakes. I squirm under his soft touch, but this simple resistance meets with the steel force of his hands, holding me in position, forbidding me to flee the sensations.

I look down at him, kneeling on the floor at my feet, and

watch as he stares into the eye of my cock, his fingers working slowly over the smooth head at the zenith of its engorgement. He strokes me with his left hand, his right trailing along the underside of my shaft, sliding through the damp hair between my legs. When his right finger touches the pucker of my anus, it does a little dance along the rim, and then suddenly, in perfect coordination with his lips, his finger enters me as my cock enters the warmth of his lips. My body bucks in response to the dual sensations and an involuntary groan escapes me.

His lips and tongue draw me in while his left hand rings the base of my cock applying gentle pressure each time his mouth slides back along my length. His right hand sets up a counter-rhythm, fucking me with growing vigor in opposition to the ministrations of his mouth. Soon I can feel the heat beginning to rise inside me, my skin burning and my eyes glazing as he works me over.

The rhythm of his hands increases, and his mouth slides and glides, faster and faster until the first shocking light of orgasm rolls up from inside me. I feel the heat rising in my stomach then my groin. In an instant, much faster than I anticipate, the feeling spills up into my cock, spurting out into his mouth with a suddenness that shocks me. He sucks harder when he feels me begin to come, holding me tight against him and drinking every drop. I lean back against the closed door behind me and breathe heavily.

In a flash he is on his feet, jerking himself off in a quick, precise motion, then turning slightly to the side so that the gushers of hot come spurt onto the cubicle wall in broad, sticky streaks. He groans, the thick and ropey veins in his forearms sliding along solid muscle, his fingers slowing to squeeze out the last of his come.

"I was going to help you with that," I say, my voice throaty and breathy, a smile sliding uselessly beneath the words.

"I know," he says, finishing up, tucking himself in with a quick precision, buttoning his pants and sliding past me to the door.

I grab my pants as he reaches for the doorknob.

"Brother for brother, Senator," he says, then smiles, taps his iPod and leaves me standing alone in the fluorescent hum of the cubicle.

I glance at my watch as I hit the stairwell. Less than thirty minutes until I meet Charlie in Grayson for the alumni meeting. I walk back across the lobby of the business school, stopping at the bulletin-vids to download a couple of flyers, an instructor list and some articles on fundamentals of wartime production statistics that I figure might provide me with a suitable excuse for having been in the building, then walk out the front door into the humid afternoon.

I walk back across the quad toward the student union, now renamed the Bush Memorial Social Center, and climb the broad steps to the revolving door. I explore the main floor until I find a soda machine, slide my card and extract a pouch of Diet Coke. I suck down half the soda in a single gulp then wander back across the broad lobby of the building and walk out the opposite side of the building onto the terrace that overlooks the playing fields.

The canvas awnings do little to block the sun this late in the afternoon, so I slide my shades back on and walk to the railing, looking down over a dozen tennis courts, a running track, and far to my left, a baseball diamond. A trio of young men running in tandem round the near corner of the track in front of me.

The tallest of the three runs slightly ahead of the others, his long muscular legs carrying him across the turf in elegant loping strides. He is shirtless, olive skinned with short-cropped fur across the bulging muscles of his legs and bare chest. He is wearing red running shorts that do nothing to hide his prodigious endowment. He has dark curly hair that cascades to his shoulders, shimmering in the evening light in voiceless rebellion against the military fashions that have invaded the campus.

A pace behind the leader, a short, compact young man in camo running shorts and a pale blue Alpha Beta tank top pounds along the innermost lane. His skin is dark, almost blue black, his head shaved close in a jarhead cut. His body is so thick and muscular that I marvel at his apparent agility. His shorts are loose, flapping side to side as he runs, the thick outline of the head of his cock clearly visible, pushing against the fabric with each stride.

To his left runs a small wiry redhead, also in an Alpha Beta tank top and camo shorts, his legs and arms pale and solid. A few tufts of strawberry blond hair peek out from the neckline of his shirt, like the promise of hidden pleasures. I imagine the fur extending from his neckline across his flat belly to the forest between his legs, strawberry fields forever.

I am letting my eyes roam over the runners' bodies when I feel a presence beside me. I slowly pivot and see Charlie standing beside me, sucking on the straw of a pouch of Coke and grinning.

My eyebrow arches, but he says nothing. He finishes his soda, crumples the empty pouch, tosses it across the terrace, free-throw style, then grins when it slices into a trash can.

"You ready, Boss?"

"I thought we were meeting at Grayson," I say.

"Just keeping an eye on you, Boss."

I stare at him for a moment, his features immobile behind his shades.

"Okay then," I reply, "let's move out, Charlie."

Charlie flashes me an inscrutable smile, thick fingers reaching up to touch his earbud.

The Alumni Advisory Committee meeting drags on for nearly ninety excruciating minutes before the chairperson finally brings the arguments to a halt and calls for a vote on the final agenda item. The vote is seven to four in favor of reopening the campus for the fall semester despite the most recent bombings that have killed a couple dozen students and staff members and destroyed the bio-tech building. The chairperson of this group sits on the Board of Regents and will represent us in their deliberations.

I fidget with my ring and watch the digital clock on my tablet.

When the meeting is over, Charlie and I walk out to the main elevators and crowd in with a group of students. He hates it when I refuse to take the secured elevators and spends the ride down with his hand on his gun.

In the lobby, Charlie and I walk purposefully across the broad marble expanse in the direction of the doors, the dark evening clearly visible through the wall of glass at the far end of the open space.

I feel Charlie's hand on my arm and, in the space of an instant, we are both thrown to the ground, Charlie rolling on top of me as the glass wall in front of us explodes in a concussion of fire, glass and smoke. Before the smoke has cleared, Charlie has his gun in his hand and has pulled me close against his body, surveying the room.

"EMP," he says tapping his earbud, "communications are down." His voice sounds as ragged as I feel, the adrenalin pumping through both of us. My muscles tense as I recognize a familiar body in tight yellow DAF shirt and camos lying lifeless near the base of the stairs. Blue eyes stare lifelessly in my direction. I am riveted by the sight of him lying there in the fallout of this terrible moment.

Charlie yanks me to my feet, eyes scanning the decimated lobby, pulling me close to him, and then hustling the two of us back into the building past the elevators to a rear exit. We stumble across the parking lot, sirens wailing and people running in all directions around us. In an instant we are both locked securely inside the dark, shielded interior of the limo.

My shirt and jacket are charred and ripped in several places. There is blood from half a dozen gashes on my hands and face. I look up at Charlie and see that he too is bloodied, his face dark from minor flash burns, a mask of pale skin where his sunglasses had been. His green eyes are wide, his breathing ragged and heavy. He looks at me and then looks down at his torn jacket and bloodied hands and laughs. His voice is unrestrained, a deep rumbling sound that I have never heard before, his eyes glinting and wrinkling around the edges.

"Fuck," he says, falling back against the cool soft leather, still laughing, "you and your goddamned public elevators!"

"Well, I knew you'd protect me," I say, relaxing back into the seat, willing the tension out of my shoulders.

"Fuck," he says again, "you are such a challenge."

I look over at him reclining on the seat beside me. His eyes are closed as he brings his breathing under control, his blond hair tousled and flecked with ash and debris. His hands, dusted with golden hair that disappears into the wrists of his jacket, are resting palms down on the dark fabric covering his muscular thighs. On the ring finger of his left hand is a ring I have never noticed before. Thick and gold, it is shaped like a traditional school ring, but in place of the stone, the Greek letters *Alpha Beta* are carved elegantly in a field of obsidian.

I look at the identical ring on my own hand and smile.

Charlie's breathing begins to slow perceptibly.

In the closed space, the smell of our sweat is strong, but not unpleasant and I find myself becoming aroused, my cock thickening against my thigh.

"What are you looking at?" he says, eyes never opening.

"Nothing."

"I saw the boy there in the lobby."

"How did you—"

He grins and opens his dazzling green eyes, turning his head to face me. "I'm your fucking bodyguard; do you imagine I don't know what you're doing at all times?"

"But—"

"I'm sorry about the boy."

"Yeah." I don't know what to say to this.

We stare at each other for a long moment then Charlie reaches out his hand and places it on my thigh, a simple gesture that reverberates through my skin to my now-throbbing cock.

"Brother for brother," he whispers.

"Charlie, I think this is the beginning of a beautiful friendship."

"Whatever you say, Boss." His hand slides up my thigh until he reaches the outline of my erection, his green eyes dancing with desire.

OFF CAMPUS, MAN

Ryan Field

Harlan LaRochelle was an attractive young man with a plan of his own. He didn't want to go to Morehouse College in Atlanta like his father and two older brothers. He'd applied to Morehouse to appease them, but then he'd secretly applied to a large university in Washington, DC.

A few months later, his father smiled and patted his back when he'd been accepted to Morehouse; his mother hugged him and cooked his favorite dinner. But when Harlan announced during that same dinner that he was going to the large university in Washington instead, his father dropped his fork so fast he chipped a dinner plate. The mother clutched her napkin and gave him a look.

Harlan looked his father in the eye without blinking. "I'm going to college in Washington, DC," he said. "I've been accepted already. They have an excellent journalism program there."

All this was true. They did have an excellent journalism department at the Washington school. But the real reason he didn't want to go to Morehouse College was because the thought of spending four more years without knowing what it was like to kiss another man caused his stomach to turn and his knees to twitch. He needed distance from his prominent Atlanta family. And he needed to explore his sexuality as much as he needed to study. He was a smart young man, with soft brown skin, a nice firm, round ass, and square, firm chest muscles. He already knew that women were attracted to him, but he wanted to find out if men were interested in him, too.

A few months after that, at the end of August, when the shouting and mean stares finally subsided, he kissed both parents good-bye, started his black SUV, and drove north to Washington.

The first few weeks he concentrated on getting settled in the dorms and focusing on his school work. His roommate was a tall, thin techie type who spent most of his time with his face glued to a computer screen. Harlan liked most of his classes and he made a few casual friends. And everywhere he went he saw good-looking young men. When he passed them by on his way to class, his penis jumped and he had to stare down at his shoes so he wouldn't get a full erection. But he wasn't sure what to do or how to approach any of them.

And then one Saturday afternoon in mid-September everything changed. He was on his way back to his room when he accidentally bumped into a guy wearing shiny red running shorts and an oversized black sweatshirt in the dormitory lobby. The guy had long, wavy, dark blond hair, was average height, and hadn't shaved in about two days. His pale blue eyes were the color of Harlan's birthstone, aquamarine. Harlan had been looking for his keys in his backpack and hadn't seen him coming. He'd bumped his elbow and had knocked all his books to the floor.

The guy smiled and said it wasn't a big deal, but Harlan went down on his knees to pick up all his books anyway. And when he was on the floor, he couldn't help noticing the guy's legs. They were covered with a soft layer of dark blond hair and you could actually see his thigh muscles pop and flex above his knees. His red shorts gathered near his crotch and made his dick round out. Evidently, he wasn't wearing underwear that day. You could see his thick cock to the right of the center seam; the outline of the head formed a visible ring.

When Harlan stood and handed him the books, the guy looked him in the eye and said, "Thanks, man. I was just on my way to the bathroom." His voice was deep and throaty, and he spoke with a New York accent. He gave Harlan a long, intense look, scratched his dick a couple of times and tilted his head toward the men's room door.

Harlan's eyebrows went up and he clenched his fists. Then he swallowed back hard and said, "Ah, well, sorry I knocked into you like that." His voice was soft and slow; he almost choked on his words.

"It's all good, man," the guy said. "I'll see you around." He scratched his dick again and looked Harlan up and down. He stared at Harlan's lips and licked his own. Then he loped to the other side of the lobby to the men's room. When he opened the door, he looked back at Harlan, tilted his head toward the inside of the bathroom a couple of times, and crossed through.

The dorms were empty on Saturday afternoons, and there was no one else in the lobby. Harlan stood there staring at the bathroom door for a few seconds, then he took a deep breath and followed the guy inside. When he passed through the doorway, he heard someone clear his throat in the last stall. It smelled like peppermint disinfectant and urine. He knew it had to be the guy with the hairy legs clearing his throat. So he crossed to the next to the last stall, pushed the door open and went inside. His hands were on the verge of shaking and his heart was racing. And when he looked down and saw that there was a hole in the wall right next to the toilet paper dispenser, he nearly choked on his own saliva. The hole was the size of a small grapefruit, and he could see the guy's hairy legs in the next stall. He was sitting on the toilet. His shorts were down around his ankles and his knees were spread apart.

Harlan dropped his backpack on the floor and pulled down his pants. Then he sat on the toilet and waited to see if the guy with the hairy legs would make the first move. The walls of the stall were covered with graphic graffiti. Phone numbers with sentences like, *I'll suck your cock, no strings attached,* were written everywhere. There were even a few articulate drawings of large, thick cocks—and one of an asshole, with an arrow attached to a sentence that read, I *need to get fucking gang-banged, guys. Fuck my hole hard.* Harlan's mouth fell open and he reached down to grab his dick. It was already semierect and it jerked when he wrapped his fingers around the shaft.

Then he heard a shuffling sound coming from the next stall. It sounded like the guy with the red shorts was standing up. A second after that, he looked down and saw the guy's black running shoes under the partition, with the red shorts still around his ankles. Harlan sat back and looked up at the hole. He couldn't see into the next stall anymore, because the hole was filled with a nine-inch erection and two low-hanging balls. It was the cock of his dreams: thick and straight and smooth, with one of those slightly pointed acorn heads. The fact that Harlan already knew that all this junk was attached to a pair of sexy, hairy legs and a rugged jaw with five o'clock shadow only made it better. He heard a sigh in the next stall, and the cock rocked up and down a few times.

Harlan reached out slowly and wrapped his hand around the wide shaft. He'd never held another man's penis in his palm before; it felt softer than he'd imagined. Then he got down on the white-tiled floor, on his knees, and slowly began to jerk the tender skin back and forth. Harlan was aware of safe sex: he didn't have any open sores or cuts in his mouth, and he wasn't going to suck him off to the finish. But he had to slip it into his mouth and taste it for a minute. He wanted to know what it was like to have that thick, smooth vein on the bottom of the shaft pressed against his tongue; he needed to inhale the smell of his sweaty, tangy balls up close. So he opened his mouth, stuck out his tongue, and wrapped his lips around the head. When he inhaled the guy's locker-room smell through his nostrils, he closed his eyes and held his breath for a moment. His eyelids fluttered and his shoulders dropped forward. It was even better than he'd imagined it to be. The guy in the next stall moaned out loud. And when Harlan slipped it slowly to the back of his throat, he heard the guy whisper, "Ah, yeah, man."

He smiled; he wanted to please him. So his cheeks indented and he began to suck him off. He'd received a few meaningless blow jobs from girls, so he knew how to do it. He grabbed his own cock; it was fully erect by then. But when he began to jerk his dick, sucking the guy off at the same time, the men's room door opened with a loud, metal screech. He heard the sound of more than one deep voice. Several guys clomped toward the urinals, joking and horsing around. Harlan's eye's opened wide and his head went back. He panicked: the guy's dick slipped from his mouth and he stood up fast. He imagined them finding him there on his knees, sucking a guy off in the men's room. He pictured the security guards handcuffing him and carting him off to the local police station where his parents would have to come and bail him out. So he pulled up his pants, grabbed his backpack, and loped out of the stall with his head bent down.

And that night, while his roommate snored, Harlan covered his dick with a dirty, white sock and jerked off in his bed under the covers. He couldn't stop thinking about the guy with the red shorts and the hairy legs; he couldn't get the taste of his perfect dick out of his mouth.

He thought about that guy's dick for the rest of the week, too. He passed by the men's room in the dorm lobby every night hoping he'd return, but that never happened. It was a large university and he figured he'd never see him again.

On Saturday night, Harlan was so frustrated he decided to do something different: it was time to check out the gay bars near Dupont Circle in Washington. He found a good parking spot on the street and went to a smaller bar first. He figured he had a better chance of getting into the small bars. He was only nineteen and you had to be twenty-one. But when he walked up to the entrance door, the hefty bouncer smiled and held out his hand for the cover charge without asking questions. He even looked him up and down, raised his eyebrows, and whistled.

The bar was dark with a low ceiling. He found an empty stool at the end, where he sat down and ordered a martini. Then he took a deep breath and sighed. It didn't seem like there were any single guys in the entire bar. Small groups of middle-aged gay men clustered together and told jokes. Couples of all ages sipped drinks and murmured softly to each other. He didn't know this at first, but to the right of him, a rough-looking young man stood staring at the back of his neck with his lips pressed together and his strong hands in his pockets. When Harlan finally looked into a cloudy mirror over the bar and saw the guy, he sat back and made believe he knew nothing.

The rough guy's face was unshaven, although his long side-burns were thick and had been narrowed with care. He bumped into the back of the bar stool with his hips, then he leaned forward slowly, pressing tight to the back of the stool. "You okay, man?" he said. "Can I buy you a drink?"

"I'm fine," Harlan said. He didn't turn around right away. His heart was beating too fast and he didn't want to stammer. But there was something familiar about the guy's voice that raised his right eyebrow.

"You sure are fine."

"Ah, well, thank you," Harlan said. He almost rolled his eyes.

The guy moved in closer, marking his territory. His crotch pressed into the back of the stool, with enough force to push it forward a fraction of an inch. Harlan turned around and reached for the back of the chair to keep his balance, but he grabbed the guy's strong forearm by accident. There was a tattoo that ran from his wrist to his elbow, with dark swirls and twists.

"I've been checking out your jeans," the guy said. He placed his wide palm on Harlan's left shoulder, as if claiming his prize. His breath smelled like beer and stale tobacco. "I like the pockets on these much better than the ones you were wearing the first time I saw you."

Harlan's eyebrows went up and he turned around to face him. "The last time you saw me?" He picked up the martini and took a large swallow. *Did he know this guy?*

The guy laughed. "Yeah, man," he said, "in the men's room in the dorm."

He picked up his drink and finished it in one gulp. It all came rushing back in flashes. The red shorts, the hairy legs, the long, thick cock, and the deep voice. But now he was wearing baggy jeans and a tight, black short-sleeved shirt. His long blond hair had been cut shorter and combed back. "Ah, well," Harlan said.

He leaned forward and whispered, "What's your name, man?"

"Harlan. What's yours?" The vodka had calmed his nerves and stopped his right leg from jerking up and down.

"Devon," he said, "but they call me Dev." He squared his shoulders. His voice was loud and firm, with a low, raspy tone.

"I can't believe I actually ran into you again," Harlan said. He knew his words were slurred. His lips felt numb and his toes were already tingling.

Dev had an awkward way of taking control...rocking on the balls of his feet, kneading his fingertips into Harlan's shoulder blade with uncalculated strokes. He bought him two more drinks and they talked for the next two hours. They both went to the same university, but he was two years ahead of Harlan. Harlan told him he was a journalism student, and he told Harlan his major was criminal justice and that his ultimate goal was to work for the FBI. He never left Harlan's side, standing so close it looked as if he were holding him prisoner. He finally rested his hand on Harlan's right shoulder and said, "It's getting close to last call. The bar is going to shut down soon."

Harlan ran his fingers up the long, spiral tattoo on his forearm. "Do you have more tattoos?" He liked tattoos; he'd always wanted one.

"All over, man," he said. "There's a long snake that goes from my belly button all the way down to my dick." Then he moved into the bar so no one could see anything, pulled down his zipper and grabbed Harlan's hand. He put his hand between his legs and shoved it into the opening of his baggy jeans. "Can you feel that snake, baby?"

He was wearing loose boxer shorts, but Harlan could feel the outline of his semierect penis; it was hanging long and heavy. He closed his eyes and took a deep breath, then said, "My room-mate went home for the weekend and I have the dorm room all to myself."

"Fuck the dorms," Dev said, "I did them my first year and hated them. Now I rent a loft off-campus, man, with a couple of other dudes. We can go there. The guys won't mind."

When they arrived at the loft, Dev opened the front door and Harlan went inside first. It was dark, but there was a small lamp burning near a window next to the door. Dev said his roommates were sleeping and he didn't want to switch on all the lights. A small dog came running to the entrance, a red toy poodle that weighed about seven pounds and had a deep, hoarse bark. The dog lunged at Harlan, sinking his teeth into his pant leg and shaking his head in half circles. "Down, Tucker," Dev shouted. "I don't know what's wrong with him. He's usually not like this." The dog stepped back and stared up at Dev. He stopped barking but continued to growl at Harlan.

Dev ignored the dog. He put his palm on Harlan's ass and squeezed it tight. "Maybe he's worried about what I'm going to do to you tonight," he said. "Maybe he knows I'm going to split you in half with this." He smiled, and then reached down and grabbed his crotch.

Harlan sighed. Even though this rough guy was all his sex fantasies come true, he was still almost a virgin and he wasn't sure how far he wanted to go that night. So he looked down at the floor and said, "I've never done this before. I've done a few things with guys, but not that much."

Dev smiled and put his arm around his waist. He kissed him on the mouth and said, "You don't have to do anything you don't want to do, baby. I'll stop whenever you want." Then he kissed him again and said, "Damn, you are beautiful."

Harlan took a deep breath and stepped past the dog. He looked around the loft. There was a large rock crystal obelisk on the glass table in the entrance area and he ran his fingers across an expensive satin pillow on a side chair. Evidently, Dev looked rough on the outside, but he had good taste in accessories. The dog glared at him and continued to growl, so Dev picked him up and said, "I'll put him up in the loft. There's a small office up there where we all study, and it has a gate."

When Dev came down from the upstairs loft a few minutes later, he was naked. Harlan was still standing in the hallway waiting. His eyes opened wide and his head jerked back.

Dev smiled. His semierect dick was swinging back and forth between his hairy legs. "Can I get you anything?" he asked.

"Ah, well, no," Harlan said. His mouth dropped and he stared at his crotch.

Dev walked up to him and kissed him on the mouth again. "Then let's go over to my bed." He took Harlan's hand and pulled him toward the other side of the loft.

But halfway there, Harlan stopped in the middle of the open room and stared down at a naked guy on a black leather sofa. His eyes were adjusting to the darkness, and the streetlights outside created a soft glow through the tall, exposed windows. The naked guy's eyes were closed and he was stretched out on his back with his legs spread wide. There was a thick, soft penis resting between his legs. His left hand was behind his head and he was holding his large balls with his right. His head jerked fast and his eyes opened. He looked at Harlan, then at Dev, and said, "I see we have company tonight, man. It's about time you got laid."

Dev smiled and placed his palm on the small of Harlan's back. "Just go back to sleep, dude. We won't make much noise."

The guy smiled and closed his eyes. When he readjusted his body, his dick bounced off his thigh.

Then Dev pulled Harlan to the other side of the room. They stepped behind a wide, Asian screen that partially divided the loft, where there were two full-sized beds backed up to a solid brick wall. The beds were separated by a long pine dresser. A large window at the foot of one bed brought in even more streetlight. Harlan looked up at the brick wall and saw a huge political poster, with a smiling photo of Barack Obama and Joe Biden. Dev's bed, the one on the left, was empty. But there was another guy sleeping in the bed on the right. The white covers were pulled up over his head, and one of his naked legs was hanging over the side of the mattress.

Harlan looked down at the guy in the bed and said, "I'm not sure about this. Won't these guys get pissed off at you for bringing *me* here?"

Dev kissed him on the mouth and said, "Relax. It's all cool, man. They bring women back all the time and I never complain."

"*Women?*"

Dev shook his head and laughed. "Yeah," he said, "These are my buddies. They're straight, but they know I'm gay and they really don't care. We have an agreement and it works." He reached down and cupped the younger man's ass hard. "And, this is the first time in a long time I've brought *anyone* back here."

Harlan looked down at the other bed. The guy's body jerked fast. When he realized there were other people in the room and one was staring at him, he pulled down the covers, lifted his head and looked at them both. When he saw that it was only Dev standing there, he scratched his balls, turned on his side, and closed his eyes again. Harlan took a deep breath and turned back to Dev. But by that time Dev was on his bed and his full erection was in his right hand.

Dev spread his legs and smiled. Everything he said from then on was in a whisper. "Why don't you get undressed and put your face between my legs," he said. "I know what you want."

Then he grabbed his dick with both hands and waved it back and forth.

Harlan smiled, then closed his eyes and took a deep breath. He wasn't sure about the straight roommates, but he wasn't going to let them ruin this opportunity. Besides, he figured he'd probably never see them again anyway. So he pulled off his clothes fast and climbed into Dev's bed. Then he rested his head on Dev's hairy thigh and said, "I think I know what you want, too."

Dev sat up higher and licked his lips. Then he grabbed his dick again and said, "Get down on your knees, bitch, and suck me off." His voice was soft, but it went deeper, and his eyes narrowed. When he'd called him "bitch," he'd smiled.

Harlan wanted to lick the dark, primal tattoos all over his thin, muscular torso. They swirled and turned down, over his shoulders and around his biceps like the scrollwork on an old wrought iron fence. There was a tattoo that looked like a black leather garter belt on his right thigh, and the long snake that ran down below his stomach had an open mouth with a forked serpent's tongue that curled up. His belly button was pierced and his pubic hair had been shaved. Harlan stared at his cock with glazed eyes and got up on his knees so he could start sucking him off.

"That's it," Dev said, "get down on your knees, fucking bitch." He seemed to know how to express the words Harlan wanted to hear without having to be told. His voice didn't waver and his aggressive attitude continued to expand.

Harlan went down and placed one hand on Dev's hard thigh and reached for his dick with the other. It was so thick he couldn't get his hand all the way around the shaft. But when he opened his mouth and pressed his wet lips to the head, he sucked it all the way to the back of his throat without gagging. Dev closed his eyes and rested back on the mattress. He spread his legs wider and ran his right hand down Harlan's back. His hand was rough; there were calluses on his palms from working out with weights that made Harlan want to spread his legs as wide as they would go. And when he did spread them, Dev reached back and pressed the tip of one finger to his anus.

His cock tasted salty and smelled like the inside of the men's locker room at the school gym. His thick finger probed and penetrated the inside of Harlan's tight hole. He sucked and slurped so hard his lips started to swell and his cheekbones hurt. This was a huge dick; he was starved.

"Suck that dick," Dev said in a stage whisper. "Slide those pretty lips up and down my dick and suck me off, bitch."

Harlan sucked harder. He'd never realized how much he liked dirty talk and taking orders from a strong man. So he continued to suck until he could taste the salty precome on his tongue. He swallowed hard and gulped. He wanted to suck him off completely, so that Dev would smile when he thought about it afterward. He had a feeling that Dev was the type who liked that sort of thing—just lying there getting sucked off without having to do anything in return.

But after a half hour of being sucked, Dev pulled his finger out of Harlan's ass and said, "I'm gonna fuck you now, buddy. You wanna get fucked?"

Harlan was a virgin in this sense. But he lifted his head and said, "Fuck me. Fuck me hard, man." When Dev said the word "buddy," his balls had tightened. This one word had the ability to cause a strong wind of erotic emotion from the depths of his stomach to the tips of his fingers.

Dev smiled and slapped his ass, then he rose up and kneeled in front of him. Harlan was still on his knees; his mouth was open and he was staring at Dev's cock. "Get up, buddy, and lay down on your stomach so I can breed that ass."

Harlan rested his body facedown on the white sheets and arched his back. When he looked to his right, the straight guy in the bed next to them was facing their direction, but his eyes were still closed.

While Harlan stretched out and prepared to be mounted, Dev reached into a small white bowl on top of the pine dresser and frowned when he found that it was empty. He got up off the bed, tapped his roommate on the shoulder and asked, "Man, I'm all out of condoms; can I borrow one of yours?"

The roommate opened his eyes, stared at Dev's erection, and said, "In the top drawer, dude. Help yourself." Before he closed his eyes again, he looked over at Harlan and said, "Have fun."

Dev opened the top drawer and Harlan smiled and spread his legs wider. He didn't care about the other guys anymore; he only cared about Dev climbing onto his back and fucking his brains out. He was somewhat worried about the initial pain. Dev's dick was enormous. But Harlan had been playing around with dildos for a while, and he knew what his hole could take.

Dev ripped the condom package open with his teeth and covered his cock fast. Then he looked down and said, "I'm gonna fuck that ass. I'm gonna fuck it hard, bitch."

The roommate snickered, and Harlan closed his eyes and arched his back higher. He wanted to feel the pain. Though he came from a strong, well-respected family in Atlanta, he liked being someone's bitch in bed now that he was off on his own in college. And Dev-the-Dude seemed to know this, too. He mounted him and spit on his dick a few times to lubricate it more. When he pressed the tip to Harlan's opening, Harlan gasped for a moment and bit the side of his fist. He felt a strong, sharp pain that made his eyes roll back. But it only lasted a second, and then Dev's cock slid to the bottom of his soft, tight hole as if it had been sized to fit. He closed his eyes and said, "Fuck me hard, man. I need to get fucked really hard."

Dev smiled. "I was wrong about you," he said, "I thought you'd be one of those tight asses that didn't like to fuck and I'd have to beg to get inside. But you're a real player. You love dick."

Harlan moaned while he fucked. He knew the guy in the bed next to them was watching everything now and he didn't care. He'd seen him open his eyes the minute Dev started fucking. Dev's cock went all the way in and he bucked his hips fast. Harlan's entire body tingled with preorgasmic sensations. His dick rubbed against the sheets; the only thing he was worried about now was coming too soon. So he bit the side of his hand and concentrated hard to make it last longer.

When Dev pressed his palms on the mattress, he straightened his arms, and started pushing his pelvis forward. It went in and out; his cock slid from the bottom of Harlan's hole back to the lips of his anus. It rubbed his prostate and he rolled his eyes; his head bobbed up and down and his toes curled. When Dev plunged as deep as he could, his huge balls slapped against the back of Harlan's ass. A drop of perspiration fell from Dev's underarm and landed on his cheek. When it dripped down the side of Harlan's face, it landed on his lips and he licked it off.

Dev fucked hard and talked dirty. He called him "bitch," "pussy-whore" and "cock slave." Harlan forgot all his inhibitions. He begged, "Fuck me, man. Fuck my tight hole, man." And after twenty minutes of nonstop slamming, Dev finally said, "I'm close, bitch. I'm gonna breed that ass."

The roommate pulled his covers off and got up. He grabbed his own erection, stared at Harlan's ass with glazed eyes and said, "Go, man. Fill that hole with seed."

Then Dev stopped fucking for a moment and said to Harlan,

"You want my straight buddy to jerk off on your face, man, while I fuck you?" Then he looked at his buddy in the next bed and smiled.

Harlan turned to his right and looked at the roommate. He was sitting on the end of his bed, jerking his dick. From what he could see, he was a short guy, with dark hair and a stocky, weightlifter's body. His dick wasn't as big as Dev's, but it was already dripping with precome. So Harlan nodded yes and closed his eyes again.

"C'mon over and blow your load on his face, buddy," Dev said. "He wants it."

Then Dev began to fuck him again.

The roommate stood and crossed to the side of the bed. He leaned forward over Harlan's face; he spread his stocky legs and started jerking off. Harlan began to moan louder. He opened his mouth and stuck out his tongue all the way; the roommate bent his knees and slapped his dick against Harlan's cheek. The harder Dev slammed his virgin ass, the higher his voice went. He banged so hard the bed moved sideways. Harlan's right leg bent at the knee and went up; his toes curled and every muscle in his body braced for climax. He reached down, shoved his hand under his body and grabbed his own cock. And when Dev finally erupted, Harlan shot a huge stream all over the sheets.

A second later, while Dev was still emptying the last of his load into the condom, the roommate grunted and jerked a hefty load all over Harlan's face. His mouth was still open and a few drops landed on his tongue. Then the roommate shook his dripping cock a couple of times, slapped it on his face, and said, "Thanks, dude." After that, he loped back to his bed and rested on top of the covers.

Dev remained inside while the roommate's come dripped down Harlan's face. He whispered dirty things into his ear and caressed the right side of his ass. Harlan liked the postorgasmic sensation of having dick in his body after the climax, slowly rubbing his tender prostate. He closed his eyes, took a deep breath and wiggled his hips. The roommate's come was strong; it smelled like bleach and tasted salty.

A few minutes later, Dev pulled out, removed the condom, and said, "You've got a great ass, baby."

Harlan wiped away the roommate's come with the side of his hand and said, "And you've got a great dick."

Dev slapped his ass and kissed the back of his neck. "I'll get you a wet towel."

When Dev got out of bed and crossed to the bathroom, Harlan licked most of the roommate's come off his hand and swallowed hard. Then he looked over and saw that the roommate was now sound asleep. He hadn't had a chance to take a good look at him that night, and he was curious. His big legs were spread wide and his thick arms were back over his head, exposing the dark patches under his arms. Then he took a closer look and his mouth opened wide. The roommate who had just given him a facial was actually in one of his journalism classes. He sat two seats away from him on Mondays and Thursdays. Harlan's eyebrows went up and he sighed. But there wasn't much he could do about it now.

Then Dev came back and dropped a warm, soapy washcloth on his back and said, "You must be tired after that work over, man. I'll bet you'll sleep great tonight."

He cleaned the rest of roommate's come off his face and smiled. It sounded like Dev had gotten what he'd needed and now he wanted him to leave. "I'm okay," he said. "I'll get dressed in a minute and go back to the dorms."

But Dev climbed on top of him again and wrapped his arms around his shoulders. His hairy legs pressed against his thighs.

"I thought you'd spend the night here, man," he said. His voice was still deep, but softer now, with an apologetic tone. "I thought you'd wake up in my arms, man. I've been thinking about you since you knocked me over that day in the dorm lobby."

Harlan tossed the wet come-rag on the floor and smiled. "I can do that. As long as you're sure your roommates won't mind me spending the night."

Dev reached down and grabbed his ass. Then he laughed and said, "I don't think they'll mind. The only thing I'm worried about now is that the dude in the bed next to us is going to try to get into your pants, too. I've never seen him so horny, man. But that's not gonna happen."

"Why?" Harlan asked. He tilted his head slantwise and pressed his lips together.

"Because that ass belongs to me now, baby," he said. Then he shoved his hairy knee between Harlan's legs and kissed him on the mouth.

KISSING THE JOY

Jeff Mann

Youth is the only thing worth having.
—Oscar Wilde, *The Picture of Dorian Gray*

It's hard not to stare. Not only because he's so beautiful, but because the semester's nearing its end. When Intro to Creative Writing finishes up in a few weeks, I may never see him again.

Openly ogling my own student, especially a straight one twenty-eight years younger than I, would be offensive, foolish, pointless and highly unprofessional, so my sidelong glances and roving gazes must suffice. While I'm talking about literary nonfiction—how much must be true, how much may be made up, how to write a braided or a lyric essay—I'm taking in Shaun's handsome looks. He's wearing madras shorts on this warm April day, revealing, much to my delight, rangy legs covered with black hair. He sprawls back in his seat, taking the occasional note. Against the front of his tight black T-shirt, I can discern the curved mounds of his chest, the flat plain of his belly. His arms are sinewy, slender but muscular: little biceps swell up when he stretches or cups his hands behind his head. From the short T-shirt sleeves, tattoos spill—dark thorns and swirls, black fires—making me wonder where else, on skin never publicly revealed, he might be marked. Those teasing glimpses of ink remind me that I'll never see him naked.

In every class this semester his eyes have been alert; he's nodded and smiled a lot. Decades of teaching have made me very conscious of such body language and expert at interpreting it: the kid obviously likes me and enjoys my class. He seems to appreciate my relaxed demeanor, my passionate palaver and dry wit. Revealing my desire for him would do nothing but frighten or disturb him. If he knew I've written several poems about him, he'd probably jog right out of here.

Class dismissed. As he does every Thursday, he gives me a big smile—very white, framed by a close-trimmed black beard I'd give sections of soul to stroke—and wishes me a great weekend. I allow myself the split-second luxury of watching his lithe form saunter out the door, backpack over his shoulder, before focusing on the inevitable student questions that linger after class.

The sound of my name wakes me. It's very dark, but I can make out his silhouette in the bedroom doorway.

"Come here, boy," I say, turning on the bedside lamp. Obediently Shaun steps into the low glow.

"Strip."

He does so, peeling off his black T-shirt and shorts, tossing them on a chair. He stands by the bed, awaiting further orders, naked save for black briefs. He's a study in snow and ebony, as those of Irish descent often are: white skin, black eyes, black beard, glossy black fur coating legs and forearms, filigrees of black hair around his nipples and navel. His tattoos add further contrast: thorny rose vines, stylized rope, and Celtic knots twine his upper arms.

From the bedside bureau I fetch a roll of duct tape. Tearing off a strip, I hand it to him. "Gag yourself."

He does so, pressing the tape over his lips. The silver stretches tautly across his bearded cheeks, the ends anchored below his ears. It will pain him quite a bit tomorrow morning, when I peel it off.

I admire him for a long minute, his athletic form standing before me, waiting to be loved and used. The differences between us—his youth, my middle age; his submission, my dominance; his leanness, my burliness; his smooth torso, my hairy chest—make the magnetism between us all that more profound.

"Show me your hole." I reach for the bureau again, this time for a tube of lube.

Shaun nods, shucking off his briefs. He turns, bends over, and cups his round asscheeks with both hands. "Closer." He shuffles backward. "Wider." He spreads his cheeks farther apart. In the lamplight, I can see his tight brown ring—like the dark heart of a poppy, a tiny whirlpool—and the cloudy hair shielding it. His ass-cleft's a valley between low hills, filled with dark fog. I grease my index finger and lube him up. He sways as I enter him, then he presses back against me, wedging my finger deeper knuckle by knuckle. I find his prostate, massaging it till he groans. I pull out, overlap my middle and index fingers, and push inside him again. He rocks on my hand; I can feel his muscles relaxing, opening up. Outside the window screen, a breeze soughs in spruce boughs.

"You want me to fuck you up the ass, boy?"

Shaun's head bobs. His asshole grips my fingers, a sticky handshake from within. A few minutes' preparation—I cuff his hands before him, rope-tether his ankles together—and my anointed captive's beneath the blankets, nestled inside my arms. Against his tape-gag he's begging to be screwed; his well-lubed butt grinds against my cock. I take him slowly, sliding carefully inside, then, at his urging, pound him harder. Within minutes, I've finished inside him; he's finished in my fist. I wipe us clean; help him shuffle to the bathroom for a piss. We spend the night curled together. In the morning, I roll him onto his belly and fuck him again. Leaving him drowsing in bed, still cuffed and gagged, I head downstairs to start coffee and prepare a big country breakfast of bacon, scrambled eggs and buttermilk biscuits.

"Hey, Professor!"

I'm on the way across campus to fetch lunch when I hear my name called. It's Shaun, in another tight T-shirt and shorts. He looks very happy to see me; he's grinning broadly and his dark eyes are positively sparkling. We shake hands, firm grip to firm grip, brief and harmless press of skin to skin. We talk about the next class assignment. I try to look calm, not hungry and stunned. I try not to imagine how sweet it would be to strip him to the waist, tie his hands behind his back, and kiss him till we're both breathless. I keep my eyes on his, despite the urge to look at the contours of his chest. Then he's off to his next class; I'm left staring at the paper birch trees coming into new leaf by the student union. As if on automatic, I enter, heading to Au Bon Pain for coffee and a sandwich.

Virginia Woolf said that writing is how a writer deals with shock. Every sight of Shaun's a shock. A notebook's my lunch companion today. I finish my sandwich, pull out a pen, and, sipping my coffee, scrawl out notes for a poem.

I've spent most of my adult life trying to figure it out: what good's a perfervid passion when it has no appropriate outlet? Yearnings that deep and futile are like acorns scattered across asphalt, breeze-blown seeds meant for soil that end up withering on hot concrete, or gold-green pollen wasted across a windshield.

Shaun's only the latest in a long line of pupils who have maddened me. Big biker Don; brooding, bearded Travis; thick-muscled James; boyish, hairy Brandon; broad-shouldered blond Drew: just a few from the last decade whose presence made both my heart and my cock heat up and throb. What do I do with my feelings for boys like that? It's not just lust; that might be easy to relieve with a few hand-strokes and Kleenex. It's admiration, fondness, paternal protectiveness, a veneration of the beautiful, all mixed up with a Top's sadism, the longing to bind, gag, hurt, hold, comfort, possess, control. Perhaps I want to tie them up because I know I can't keep them, that soon enough, untouched by me, they'll pass out of my life. What they leave behind is of my making, not theirs. Fantasies, poems, essays, fiction.

William Blake was right, I suppose, when he wrote, "He who binds to himself a joy / does the winged life destroy. / But he who kisses the joy as it flies / lives in eternity's sunrise." What choice is there, as much as I would like to seize this spring's joy, bind Shaun's body, will and freedom? I either savor his beauty briefly and from a distance, or I'm arrested for abduction, kidnapping or rape. In some other world, I pull a knife, push him over the hood of my pickup truck, cuff him, tape his mouth and shove him into the cab. In some other world, force is unnecessary, for he's more than willing.

Today, a rainy mid-April afternoon, I can smell Shaun's cologne. I lean against the wall discussing Blake's poetry, and Shaun sits a few feet from me, exuding a strong scent of lime and evergreen. Normally I despise colognes, much preferring the sweaty natural musk of a man, but the source of this aroma is

so visually intoxicating in and of itself that I savor whatever
scents I can, rising off skin I cannot touch. Seeing and smelling
are permitted; touching and tasting are verboten. At the same
time that I'm pointing out the poet's use of specific imagery, I'm
noting the shiny black fur that coats Shaun's forearms. When
he bends forward to make a note, I can see the white skin of his
nape, the buried impression of his spine, the feathery dark muss
that indicates that he's due for a haircut.

How would he feel if he knew how I felt, if I told him that
I'm half in love with him, that I dream of roughly possessing
him? Would he be flattered? Horrified? Disgusted? It's a burden
to conceal the fire I feel, behind casual gestures, friendly smiles.
It's a great weight. Such meticulous masks, such constant lies.
His departure at the class period's conclusion is a loss, an ache,
and a relief.

A Facebook stalker, yes. I'd try to "friend" him so as to have
access to his photos—always the hope that I might find a shirtless pic—but that might look suspicious. The one tiny photo I
can see is mere fodder for frustration: Shaun in a black tank top.
I download it. Occasionally, I click on it, staring at his tattooed
arms, the smooth skin of his chest above the low-cut tank top
collar. How badly I want to see his nipples.

Some men share years with their beloveds. I have Shaun twice
a week, Tuesdays and Thursdays, for fifteen weeks, the length
of a semester.

So your partner's going to be gone for the week, Sir? It's Shaun
on Instant Messenger, eager for his upcoming captivity.

Yep, I type. *He's got business meetings in DC. Drive on over
on Monday. Bring some beer. We'll grill hamburgers. Are you
sure you're ready for those dungeon scenes you asked for?*

Shaun: *Yes, indeed. They sound awesome! I can take more than you think.*

Shaun's so much smaller that I worry sometimes about hurting him. His build's a gymnast's or a dancer's. Mine's a wrestler's or a quarterback's gone to seed. On the other hand, I love indulging his specific requests, and, over the six months of our affair, he's developed a real yearning for rough treatment.

Jeff: *All right. We'll start with paddling. I'm going to muzzle you, tie you over the preacher-curl bench, and spank you first with the leather paddle and then the wooden one.*

Shaun: *Cool! Mark me up, Sir. Make me cry!*

Jeff: *Count on it. Then I'm going to string you up to the ceiling pipe and take the riding crop to your back. Give you some bruise-black wings.*

Shaun: *Awesome! Keep talking, Sir. I'm really hard here.*

Jeff: *Turn on your webcam.*

Shaun obeys. There on my laptop screen is my handsome boy, that brilliant grin. He's wearing a black tank top, his dark hair half-concealed by a white baseball cap worn backward.

Jeff: *Take off your tank top. Good. Stand up. Drop your shorts. Good boy. Stuff a sock in your mouth. Good boy. Play with your tits for me, Shaun. Make them hurt a little. Good, good. Twist and tug, yep. When they start to ache, then you'll have my permission to jack off.*

I'm settled, I'm happy. Relatively happy. Doug and I have been together for fifteen years. We're not so much passionate as comfortable, like most couples together so long. We share a beautiful house, good meals, summer vacations overseas, several cats, sex both vanilla and infrequent, plus an occasional play-partner from out of town. Our kitchen's just been remodeled: sage green walls, granite counter tops. In winter, I read and write by the fire. In spring, hyacinths and daffodils bloom in the front flowerbed; the Bradford pear blossoms make a globe of white flame. In summer, we grill out on the back deck; rabbits lope over the lawn. In autumn, we rake leaves; mountains above the town turn orange and maroon. It's the kind of life I dreamed of in my youth but never thought I'd have.

Sometimes I get tired of domesticity's routines—grocery shopping, cooking and laundry—but I love our life; I know I'm very lucky. I prize the peace, the midlife stability, the calm, two solid paychecks, and a king-size bed. Doug's my Apollo, golden god of civilization and order. Still, like most professional couples our age, we're both overworked. We spend more time with our laptops than with each other. We don't touch each other the way we used to. This is to be expected, I tell myself. Lately, when I wake at night, can't fall back to sleep, I imagine Shaun, my slender, black-bearded Dionysus, in bed beside me. He's naked, impatient ass already lubed up. Rolling onto his back, he wraps his arms around his thighs, hoists his legs in the air, and begs me to take him. I bend him double; our bearded lips mingle; his ankles graze my ears; his asshole's tight as a fist. I use him hard; I come inside him. Rising, I shuffle stiffly to the bathroom, grab a wash rag, wipe myself off. Doug's still snoring when I get back to bed.

While Doug mows the lawn, I'm searching for a boy online. Someone young and hot, like Shaun. But someone gay, submissive, and into leather-sex, unlike Shaun. I check out Bear 411, Bondage Recon. I get messages, most of them from men far away. They want to be treated like slaves, like kidnap victims, forced to endure extended bondage scenes. Exactly what I'm looking for in a bottom. Except, with few exceptions, "They're all geezers!" I snarl, examining their photos. "Fuck it!" I close my eyes and see Shaun, naked, on his knees, chain and padlock around his neck, waiting for orders. He's what everyone wants to be, everyone wants to devour: young, lean, handsome, muscular. I open my eyes and see the online pics. Old men. Which is to say, my age or older. Ugh. Who would want them?

And what if I met online a bottom as beautiful as Shaun? One who shares my erotic predilections, who desires me as badly as I desire him? An otter or cub who wants a Daddy Bear to own him, rope and gag him, hurt him, protect and care for him? Would I fall stupidly, completely in love, as I did when I was single, and beautiful men wild and dark as Dionysus made a fool of me, broke my heart? Would I do as my father did twenty years ago, obsessed with a woman half his age, so deeply in love he wrecked his marriage and his family? One night we confronted him when he came home late. He called my mother a bitter old bitch. I threw a wine glass against the wall. My mother, in her cups, snarled, "There's no fool like an old fool."

I'm turning fifty this August. Doug and I are going to the Aran Islands, to the Inner and Outer Hebrides. I expect to drink a lot of good stout and scotch, eat a lot of lamb, potato cakes, black pudding, and haggis. These are not impossible pleasures. I have the currency to afford them. The mountains of Skye, the cliffs of Inishmore, the Standing Stones of Callanish: lovely landscapes— windswept, stern, cold—will help me forget human loveliness. I will dip my foolish hands into the cold Atlantic, stroke the rocky shingle, lift my face into hard sea wind.

We call it the Jesus-Truss. It's one of Shaun's favorites.

While Doug's been in DC the last few days, Shaun's been my willing captive, content comrade, and eager slave. We've played guitar together, his electric to my acoustic. We've watched a few movies, nestled together on the couch. We've lifted weights, biked on the New River Trail. And we've shared several rough scenes, the evidence of which blots my boy's biceps, buttocks and back.

Warm afternoon radiance streams over him, here in the guest bedroom. Beyond the window, the sunlit pear tree is full of brilliant blooms, a white even purer than Shaun's smooth nakedness. He's tied to the bed in the very position Christ assumes in depictions of the crucifixion, tattooed arms tied in a taut V over his head, wrists roped to the bedposts, feet crossed and ankles bound together, secured to the bed frame. A long strip of soft black leather is wrapped around his head, over his eyes; another long black strip is threaded several times between his white teeth. He's been tied this way for an hour; at first he fretted, tugging on his bonds, tossing his head. Then, weary with late nights and early mornings—I can't stop working his tits and asshole, so both of us are short on sleep—he slipped into a nap.

I read Blake in an armchair by the window, lifting my face from the book to study my bound-down, black-bearded savior so sweetly sacrificed for me. He's like spring ephemera, wildflowers blooming on the forested mountains surrounding us: bloodroot, mayapple, Solomon's seal, bluebell, ladyslipper, dog's-tooth violet. Soon enough we'll part forever. Soon enough his beard will gray like mine, his body will thicken like mine, he will join the endless generations eroded by age, falling farther and farther from perfection. But today he is spring, he is mine. Later, he will wake to my teeth's ardor on his nipples and neck, as I leave bruise after bruise. I will clamp his tits with tweezers, torture them till he weeps. I'll rope up his cock and balls, suck him off, jack off on his face and chest, rub my cooling juice into his beard. But now I'm content to read, to sit in silence and sunlight, breathe in his scents of forest and citrus, study the black puffs of fur in his armpits, about his sleep-limp cock.

* * *

I'm grading student journals. I read his first. As disobliging as reality is, there are no entries about his desperate desire for his creative writing teacher, his enthusiasm for leather bars, his admission that he's a bondage bottom. No, just well-written pages about his favorite musicians, none of whom I've heard of, plus descriptions of his travels in Central America. All less than revealing, thoroughly, disappointingly, innocuous. It isn't until I get to another student's journal, next to last in a pile of twenty, that I discover another of Sadist God's cruel jokes on me. A little blonde who sits in the back of Shaun's class has slept with him. Their enthusiasm for heavy metal music and marijuana led them together; they flirted via text-messaging, thumbs flying over the cell phone buttons. They met for pizza, got drunk, headed over to her apartment, fucked. (And how, it occurs to me as I read her confession, could I long tolerate a lover from a generation so addicted to bad music and electronic toys? Besotted as I am, how could such love last, abraded daily by the fine irritants of a chasm-wide generation gap? As if I'll ever be in her position, any position to find out.)

She's heartbroken, poor thing. Afterward, he'd fled from her bed, hasn't returned her calls, avoids her now. She's going to be glad when the semester's over and she doesn't have to face that twice-a-week reminder of how handsome he is, how badly he treated her. She's even written a sonnet about what a prick he is.

For just a second I contemplate crazy possibilities. I could pull her aside after our next class, console her, point out how fickle and flighty college boys are. Then I could ask her how big his dick is, if his ass is hairy, what tattoos he bears other than the ones I can see. She's twenty, slight, pretty, blonde, buxom, often dressed in shades of pink. I'm forty-nine, burly, silvery bearded, often dressed in cowboy boots, Everlast hoodies, jeans. A boy attracted to her, however drunkenly and temporarily, would never in a million years be attracted to me. In that realm of feeling, for him I do not exist. I am a voice, not a body. I am an email message reminding him of class readings, a scribble of approval in the margins of his journal, writing, *This makes sense, Well done!* or *I can relate.* I have heard of this from those who've preceded me into the forties and fifties: the invisibility of the middle-aged, when whatever talents or charms remain avail a man less and less.

Shaun and I both have Black Irish blood. I want to take my young lover to the Emerald Isle to celebrate our first five years together. We'll tap our toes to Celtic music in Doolin, take in grand, windswept views of the ocean from the Cliffs of Moher, visit Newgrange and the Burren, kiss the Blarney Stone, lie together naked in a narrow bed under the twilit eaves of an Inishmore inn, watching sea wind whip clouds across the skylight. My beard will be entirely gray by then; his beard will be showing first silver on the chin. I'll ease inside him come moonrise; he'll bite the pillow, groaning with happiness, his ass stuffed full; we'll fit together as smoothly as continents once did.

This scene's set in the shower stall of my basement gym. Shaun's lean arms circle the chair back, his hands shackled behind it. The heavy links rattle as I wrap chain around him, securing his torso and arms to the slats. I spread his thighs, padlocking his ankles to the chair's back legs. There's a short wooden dowel tied in his mouth. He grits his teeth, shakes his head, and drools copiously. Soon his eyes' drip joins his mouth's, as I add clothespin after clothespin to his nipples and arched pecs, his belly's ridgeline, his inner thighs, stiff cock, and lust-tight balls. When I'm finished, I hold his bowed head against my hip and let him sob.

"Endure this an hour, all right?" I grip his thick hair and pull his head up, back. His black eyes well. Tears roll down his cheeks, glittering like the several silver hoops in his ears. "For me, my little *eromenos*? You gonna make me proud?"

He nods, sobs subsiding to whimpers. Off his chin I wipe a clear string of slobber, lick it off my hand. I piss all over his chest and belly, the rank smell melding with strong aromas his armpits have brewed over the several days I've denied him a shower. I leave him there, shivering, suffering. We both know his pain and powerlessness will make dinner more delicious, wine more intoxicating, a bath more soothing balm. Freedom and tenderness will be the objects of his bit-muffled prayer, gifts begged for, at long last received.

Early May, final day of class. I give Shaun one last look as he bends over the teaching evaluation, admiring his thin but defined arms, his long, hairy legs. Silently I wish him grand luck, irrepressible passions that find myriad satisfactions, someone who will adore him as deeply as I could have, given more congenial circumstances.

A week later, Doug and I are having dinner at Arnaud's in New Orleans, with an editor interested in publishing my next collection of poems. "Why do you waste your time writing erotica? Why don't you stick to poetry?" they both want to know, since they're tired of hearing me whine about the diminutive size of my literary reputation and think that erotic fiction is a waste of my time and talent.

I'm very drunk on loads of vodka and cranberry, with a Sazerac on top of that, but I still have sufficient self-control not to say what I want to say. I don't say: *In words I make things happen that happen nowhere else. I make precious amalgams that have never occurred before. What I create is far*

less substantial than the world but far more faithful. A naked
black-bearded boy bound like Christ to my bed. Soft black
leather strips blindfolding and gagging him. The smell of him,
his fur-thick armpits. Sun pouring over his momentary youth
like momentary grace; pear petals, whiter than his flesh lit up
by sun, flaking apart and drifting along a mountain wind. The
soft sounds he makes napping. The way his happiness comple-
ments mine. Would you deny me this, this paltry only way of
possessing him? What I say is: "I'm standing in need of some
bread pudding. How 'bout y'all?"

It's an October night; a thunderstorm rolling in, ten years after
Shaun was my student. I'm in my office very late. I'm fifty-nine,
far too grizzled now for anyone to find appealing, a fact I've had
to face, a face I've grown sadly accustomed to. There's a knock
on the door. I open it, and there's Shaun. His jacket's spotted
with rain. Gray sprinkles his beard and his temples. He's put on
bulk, broader everywhere. He's as amazing as ever.

"Hello, Sir," he says, grinning. "Here I am again. You're
holding up pretty damned well. Do you have a few minutes to
spare?"

I pull him in and lock the door. I turn off the light but leave
the window blinds open so we can watch the storm. Then I
shove him against the wall with a thud. We grapple, mouths
interlocking, tongues exploring. I slip my hands up his sides,
shuck off his jacket, pull his shirt over his head. "Oh, yeah," he
sighs as I turn him around and pull rope from my desk.

Hands tied behind his back, he's on his knees, deep-throating
me. He gags a little, licks his lips, takes a deep breath, then
gulps me in again. His tongue tickles my glans, zigzags down
my shaft. I lie back in the desk chair, pants around my ankles,
hands behind my head, and watch lightning flash, filling the

window with split-second white, silhouetting building angles across the quad. I pat his bobbing head, trace the tattoos across his shoulder blades. His saliva oozes down my shaft.

Lifting him by his elbows, I kiss him, tasting and smelling my crotch on his lips. From the desk I fetch a ball gag. He grunts as I stuff the rubber sphere in his mouth, knotting the cords behind his head. "Keep quiet now," I whisper, bending him forward over the edge of the desk. Obedient, he lies there, where my laptop usually rests. Kneeling behind him, I pull off his shoes, his jeans and briefs; I beard-graze his buttocks, nipping here and there. I palm-pry his cheeks apart, flicking my tongue over his taint, up and down his crack, around his asshole and then into it. I spread his opening with my thumbs, burrowing deeper. This blessed taste, yes, and these soft moans, here's the ambrosia that makes me young again.

He's so ready it only takes a few palmfuls of spit. I enter him with great care, gingerly, fearful I'll hurt him, but there's no hurt, only his hands scrabbling against my belly, his jerky nods. Gripping his shoulders, I hold him down, my hips thrusting against him, my cock deep inside. Lightning flashes again, thunder crashes, the panes drum and stream. I pound him, I pound him. The desk drawers rattle. When the desk begins noisily bumping the wall, I help him up, only to lower him to the floor. He lies on his belly, legs spread wide. I slide on top, position my cock-head against his wet hole. Hungrily, he bucks back against me. I slip inside, bite his neck, wrap my arms around him, and begin again.

We're done. Piles of paper and toppled stacks of books scatter the floor; I've shot up his ass, he's shot across the carpet. Pretty soon he'll go his way, back to some distant life, and I'll go mine, back home to Doug. For now, it's just sweet to lie here together. I unknot his gag, untie his hands. He snuggles his bare back against my hairy chest, obviously glad to be sheltered and cherished inside my big arms.

"You came back yet again," I say, loving the weight of his head on my biceps.

"I'll always come back, in this form or some other, until you forget me, until the invitations end. I'm faithful, remember?"

I nod, pulling him closer, awash with gratitude. We'll drowse together like this, my beard brushing his nape, my fingers fondling his nipples, till the last lightning flashes, the last thunder growls, the long storm finally subsides.

GLORY HOLE SURPRISE

Shane Allison

It was colder than a dead man's dick in the bathroom. I was sitting on the toilet with my loose fits down around my ankles, and a hard-on from hell as I sat browsing through some skin mag that had been left on the bathroom floor by someone before me. *Eight Cock-Gobbling Twinks on the Prowl* it read. Things were slow 'cause school was out and the students had gone home. Summer had descended upon this small college town. But there was always some college trade lingering around, a few left behind looking for action, and me longing to wrap my lips around a high hard one. I flipped open my cell phone to check the time. *8:28* it read. Five fucking hours I had been waiting for dick.

There were only a few men that strolled in, the usual dick-teasing regulars with their high-hung nuts and uncut Vienna sausage–size dicks. Most of the dudes were too chickenshit to mess around. I usually hung out at the mall tearooms, but they had been closed for weeks due to some remodeling. I hated the thought of them tearing out the fiberglass stalls that were gutted with glory holes I had made, and replacing them with impenetrable metal ones.

My legs were falling asleep after sitting for so long. I set the porno periodical off in a corner and stood up in an attempt to wake my feet out of their slumber. I fingered my dick as I read the graffiti on the walls: LOVE TO SUCK AND FUCK, LEAVE DATE AND TIME TO MEET. TAP FOOT FOR BLOW JOB. A pearl of precum oozed from my piss slit. I smeared it along with my thumb. So horny. I fantasized of being surrounded by a gang of frat boys, their dicks hanging out of zippers of cargo shorts, and me giving proper attention to every one of them.

Suddenly, I heard the bathroom door being pushed open. It scared the hell out of me. I sat back down on the toilet, heard the clack of shoes making their way across dirty brown tile. The stranger took the stall next to mine. I peeked through the glory hole. I could make out his shirt, a set of hairy legs, but not his face. He was clever about hiding his identity. He leaned back against the wall to show me his dick and balls: nice, with a thick head, hung. I leaned back. The metal pipes of the toilet bit into my spine. He stared in at me through the hole, licking his lips. I rose up off the toilet and eased my dick through the hole. Immediately I felt fingers, then a wet warmth. His mouth. I pressed my face and hands against the partition as he sucked me off. I love getting good head. I pivoted my hips into his talented mouth. Slurps echoed throughout the tearoom. "Suck it, slut."

Talking dirty has always turned me on. I didn't want to nut too soon. So I retracted my dick, dripping with his spit, out of the hole and sat down on my commode. He looked in at me, licking his lips, jacking off. I smeared my index finger along the glory hole signaling him to give it to me. It was my turn. I watched him as he turned to face me. The buckle from his belt clanged against the floor. He worked his dick through. It was fat, veined and uncut. I slid back the tender foreskin to expose a big deep piss slit. I licked along it, slid my tongue under his musky dick, suckled the head. It grew tight in my mouth as I eased fingers up and down the shaft.

My glasses grazed against the partition. I took them off and laid them on top of the tissue dispenser. I heard him moan as I blew and I slid down off my toilet and sank to my knees. I gagged a little. Who was he? A student, a professor, one of the studmuffin janitors that swept and mopped the hallway floors every evening?

Just as things were getting good, we heard the door. He quickly pulled his dick out of my mouth, through the glory hole. We sat back on our toilets, still and quiet as we listened to whomever it was walk up to one of the urinals. I stood up and peeked over the door of my stall to see some guy with bed-messy brunet hair wearing a T-shirt and basketball shorts. The anonymous cruiser and I were holding strong, toying with our dicks to keep them hard.

The brunet peed and flushed, never did wash his hands. Before he was out of the shitter good, the stranger stood up and gave me his dick, but I didn't take up where I left off. I wanted to know what his piece felt like up my ass. I sucked his dick a little bit to let him know I was still into it, then I turned around. His dick grazed against my ass. I pulled apart both halves of my butt and pressed back until I felt the head of his dick at my hole. I reached back with one hand and worked his dick in slowly. It kept slipping out.

I attempted to take it again.

"Push in," I said. It hurt a little.

I held on to the metal rail that ran across the other side of the partition as he thrust.

Sweat started to pour down my face, between my lips. His

dick kept sliding out. I worked it in again. I spat in my hand and slathered it on my dick. His cock slid in and out of me easily. He grunted as he fucked me nasty. I came hard on the wall of the stall. Cum dripped on the floor. I didn't want him to stop. He was loud, coming close. I held on. Took his dick like a porn star. I slid off his prick. He let loose, coming on the floor, a little of it on my jeans. I unfurled some tissues and wiped my face and butt. Cum oozed like syrup from the edge of his cock.

"Damn, you can fuck." He didn't respond to my compliment. He pulled up his slacks, shoving his dick back into underwear. He flushed his toilet again and exited. I wanted to see this guy. I had to know who it was. When I peeked over my stall door, I couldn't believe it. Holy fuck! It was him: Dr. Carr, my black lit teacher from the past semester who had given me a hard time about my research papers, who announced the first day of class that we were to call him Dr. Carr because he'd earned it. He was married with a one-year-old daughter. I watched him dry his hands, checking himself out in the mirror. I quickly sat back on my toilet and waited for him to leave. I left twenty minutes after he exited.

Days after the fuck, he was set to give a speech on the poetry of Phyllis Wheatley. I attended. I sat in the auditorium thinking of his lips, and the prime, hot fucking he had given me. I thought how I could use what I knew to my advantage.

That next day, I went to his office. I peeked through the slit of window in the door. Dr. Carr was sitting grading papers. I knocked.

"Come in."

"Hi, Dr. Carr."

"Mr. Allison, what can I do for you?" He was his arrogant, usual self. I took a seat in front of him, feeling cocky knowing I had something on his ass.

"Oh, there's plenty you can do for me," I said. I looked at him without batting an eyelash.

"I know it was you."

"What are you talking about?"

"Yesterday in the bathroom."

Dr. Carr looked at me and knew what I meant.

"So where'd you learn to suck dick like that?"

"Jesus, keep your voice down."

"You had no idea it was me?"

"What do you want?" he asked.

"That *D* you gave me on the final? Well, my GPA took a real beating."

"I can't change your grade. They've already been turned in."

"That's too bad. Guess I'll have to tell your wife about what a good dick sucker you are."

"You stay the fuck away from my wife."

"I'll be applying to grad schools soon, and I can't have a *D* on my record."

"And if I refuse?

"Then I guess I will let your wife in on your extracurricular activities."

"And that's all you want?"

"I wanna suck your dick."

"Fuck you!"

"Just a few days out of the week."

"For how long?"

"Until I'm tired of you. I haven't decided."

Dr. Carr stared out of the window knowing his ass was caught between a rock and a hard place.

"Do we have a deal?"

"You need to leave. I'm an ass hair away from ripping your throat out."

"See you tomorrow, *Dr.*"

ABOUT THE
AUTHORS

DAVID AMMER is the author of more than fifty published tales of male/male love and lust. His first story appeared in *Torso* magazine in 1996, and since then his erotica has been seen in magazines worldwide, as well as in anthologies and online.

GAVIN ATLAS lives in Houston with his boyfriend, John. He has been published in anthologies from Ravenous Romance (*How the West Was Done*), Alyson Books (*Ultimate Gay Erotica 2009, Island Boys*) and Cleis Press (*Hard Hats, Surfer Boys*). His short story "La Playita" (Lethe Press) is available on All Romance Ebooks. He can be reached at www.GavinAtlas.com.

RACHEL KRAMER BUSSEL (www.rachelkramerbussel.com) has edited numerous books, including Lammy finalists *Up All Night* and *Glamour Girls: Femme/Femme Erotica*, plus *Best Sex Writing 2008, 2009* and *2010*. Her writing appears in *Best Gay Erotica 2009, Backdraft: Fireman Erotica, Quickies 3* and more than a hundred other explicit anthologies. She hosts In the Flesh Reading Series.

TOM CARDAMONE is the author of the erotic fantasy novel, *The Werewolves of Central Park,* the short-story collection, *Pumpkin Teeth,* and editor of the anthology, *The Lost Library: Gay Fiction Rediscovered.* You can read more about him and his fiction at www.pumpkinteeth.net.

H. L. CHAMPA's writing has been published in numerous places, including *Bust Magazine,* anthologies like *Tasting Him, Frenzy, Men in Shorts, Sweaty Sex, Like Magnets, We Attract* and online at Clean Sheets, Oysters and Chocolate, and Good Vibrations. More at heidichampa.blogspot.com.

RYAN FIELD is the author of the gay romance novels, *An Officer and His Gentleman* and *Pretty Man.* His short stories have appeared in books by Cleis Press, Alyson Books, STARbooks Press, Ravenousromance.com, and Loveyoudevine.com. For more information regarding his work check out www.ryanfield.blogspot.

Although **JAMIE FREEMAN** resides in North Florida, he once attended a small university in Washington, DC, that was nothing like the campus in his story. He is hard at work on more stories in his alternate future series, so stay tuned. He can be reached by email at JamieFreeman2@gmail.com.

WILLIAM HOLDEN is the author of more than thirty stories of gay short fiction. He has served as fiction editor for *RFD* magazine, authored five bibliographies for the American Library Association's GLBT Round Table and written various encyclopedia articles on the history of gay fiction and literature. He can be contacted by visiting his website, www.WilliamHoldenOnline.com.

JEFF MANN's published two books of poetry, *Bones Washed with Wine* and *On the Tongue*; a collection of memoir and poetry, *Loving Mountains, Loving Men*; a book of essays, *Edge*; and a volume of short fiction, *A History of Barbed Wire*, winner of a Lambda Literary Award.

SEAN MERIWETHER has published more than sixty short stories in venues including *Best of Best Gay Erotica 2*, *Best Gay Love Stories 2006* and *Lodestar Quarterly* as well as a collection of short fiction and erotica, *The Silent Hustler*.

NEIL PLAKCY is the author of *Mahu*, *Mahu Surfer*, *Mahu Fire* and *Mahu Vice*, mystery novels which take place in Hawaii. *Publishers Weekly* called *Mahu Fire* "Engrossing... a sharp whodunit," and the book has received enthusiastic reviews from *Library Journal*, *Out*, and many mystery and GLBT websites. Connect with him at www.mahubooks.com.

ROB ROSEN, author of *Sparkle: The Queerest Book You'll Ever Love* and *Divas Las Vegas*, has contributed, to date, to more than fifty-five anthologies, most notably the Cleis Press collections *Truckers*, *Best Gay Romance* (2007, 2008 and 2009), *Hard Hats*, *Backdraft*, *Surfer Boys*, *Bears* and *Special Forces*. Visit him at www.therobrosen.com.

SIMON SHEPPARD is the editor of the Lambda Award–winning *Homosex: Sixty Years of Gay Erotica* and *Leathermen*, and the author of *In Deep: Erotic Stories; Kinkorama: Dispatches from* the Front Lines of Perversion; Sex Parties 101 and Hotter Than Hell and Other Stories. He hangs out at simonsheppard.com.

NATTY SOLTESZ (bacteriaburger.com) has recently been published in the anthologies Best Gay Erotica 2010 and Best Gay Romance 2010, cowrote the upcoming porn film Dad Takes a Fishing Trip with director Joe Gage, and is a faithful contributor to the Nifty Erotic Stories Archive. He lives in Pittsburgh with his lover.

AARON TRAVIS's first erotic story appeared in 1979 in Drummer magazine. Over the next fifteen years he wrote dozens of short stories, the serialized novel Slaves of the Empire, and hundreds of book and video reviews for magazines. His stories have also been translated into Dutch, German and Japanese. His web page is located at stevensaylor.com/AaronTravis.

ROB WOLSHAM is twenty-two years old and lives in Lubbock, Texas. His work has appeared in the anthologies Boy Crazy: Coming Out Erotica and I Like It Like That: True Stories of Gay Male Desire. Enter his West Texas Hell at wolfshammy. com.

LOGAN ZACHARY is a mystery writer living in Minneapolis, MN. His erotica can be found in Hard Hats, Ride Me Cowboy, Taken By Force, Surfer Boys, Ultimate Gay Erotica 2009, Best Gay Erotica 2009, Boys Caught in the Act, Service with a Smile, and Unmasked II.

ABOUT
THE EDITOR

SHANE ALLISON is the proud editor of *Backdraft: Fireman Erotica* and *Hot Cops: Gay Erotic Stories*. He is the author of six chapbooks of poetry: *Ceiling of Mirrors, Cock and Balls, Black Fag, I Want to Fuck a Redneck, Eros in a Tea Room*, with *I Want to Eat Chinese Food Off Your Ass* being his most recent. His poems and stories have graced the pages of *Spork Magazine, New Delta Review, Mississippi Review, New York Quarterly, Ultimate Gay Erotica, Tie Me Up, Don't Tie Me Down, Boys Caught in the Act, Service with a Smile, Best Black Gay Erotica, Fastballs, Hustlers, Best Gay Bondage, Bears, Leathermen, Surfer Boys* and *Best Gay Erotica 2007, 2008* and *2009*. His new book of poems, *Slut Machine*, is forthcoming from Rebel Satori Press.